Plain Deception

Tara Randel

Annie's®
AnniesFiction.com

Books in the Amish Inn Mysteries series

Library of Congress-in-Publication Data
Plain Deception / by Tara Randel
p. cm.
I. Title
                      2015958696

AnniesFiction.com
(800) 282-6643
Amish Inn Mysteries™
Series Creator: Shari Lohner
Series Editor: Shari Lohner
Cover Illustrator: Kelley McMorris

10 11 12 13 14 | Printed in China | 9 8 7 6 5

1

Liz Eckardt paused in her gleaming modern kitchen, the rich scent of freshly brewed coffee in the air and the happy sound of her bed-and-breakfast guests erupting in shared laughter. A smile curved her lips. Liz had surprised everyone, including herself, when she'd bought the Victorian-style Olde Mansion Inn. Transitioning from a successful patent attorney in Boston to an innkeeper in Amish country had been a stretch, but she'd loved every minute of it—from the challenge and pride of ownership to getting to know the people in Pleasant Creek, Indiana. And once the initial excitement of opening her B&B had died down, Liz settled nicely into country life.

With only five guests currently booked at the inn, breakfast was calm this Monday morning. Even so, finding her footing as an innkeeper kept Liz's mind, as well as her body, busy. This new lifestyle had even affected her wardrobe. A practical bib apron covered a yellow blouse and blue pants. Sensible, flat shoes kept her comfortable. It was a far cry from the power suits and heels of Liz's former life. Some days it felt like the only constant was her dark blond hair, which she'd kept in long layers, shoulder-length since law school. Her home and profession might have changed, but Liz didn't want to completely replace her former life.

Sarah Borkholder, one of Liz's two part-time employees, bustled into the kitchen, wiping her hands on the apron that covered her modest gray dress that was typical wear for the Amish in the area. "Mr. Hastings wants to know if you have any more cinnamon bread."

"At the rate he's going, the man will end up with a stomachache."

Her guests, for the most part, so far had been engaging and friendly, which certainly helped her stress levels. Still, getting up at the crack of dawn to prepare breakfast for everyone took some getting used to. The muttering under her breath as Liz slipped out of bed each morning had dwindled in the weeks after she'd reopened the inn that had been closed by the previous owners. It had taken a while for zero dark thirty to become a natural part of her inner alarm clock.

Liz directed Sarah to the cinnamon bread and then set about pouring fresh coffee into a carafe. Turning toward the dining room with the full carafe in hand, she noticed Beans's full food dish. The English bulldog had been part of the package when she'd purchased the inn, something she only found out after the fact. Liz had quickly fallen in love with him, so in one fell swoop she became the owner of an inn and a pet—a pet whose lusty appetite kept her in steady kibble bills.

"Sarah, did you let Beans in this morning?"

"No." The young woman glanced at the full dish. "Usually he has eaten by now."

"He went out earlier, but with breakfast keeping us busy, I didn't get a chance to let him back in either." Carafe still in hand, Liz hurried through the utility room to open the door, expecting to find Beans camped out on the side patio. "Strange. He's not here."

Sarah's brows rose. "He must be on quite an adventure. That dog *never* misses a meal."

Liz scanned the yard. "Beans!" she called out. The plump, brown-and-white dog was nowhere to be seen. "I guess he'll be back when he's hungry."

Sarah laughed. "Which should be anytime now."

Liz nodded, still worried. Beans had his own strict schedule, largely based on his stomach, whether it needed food, belly rubs, or his soft rug to rest on. And he rarely strayed from that schedule. She took one last look around outside before closing the door and following Sarah into the dining room.

Liz was thrilled she'd been fortunate enough to hire the Amish teen when she opened the inn. Six guest rooms plus common areas, bathrooms, and cooking made for a busy day. The girl worked as hard as anyone she'd ever met, which said volumes since Liz had a lot of experience with long hours while running her own law firm. Hard work and stress had been part of her life back then.

But here in Pleasant Creek, she'd begun to relax, enjoy life, and learn to cook without burning a thing . . . most of the time. It was all because of a diary she'd inherited after her mother had passed away—a diary that had changed Liz's life by revealing a hidden part of her mom's past.

Liz had been raised in Boston by her widowed mother and always assumed they were alone in the world, until the diary steered her to Indiana in search of her mother's Amish roots. In Pleasant Creek, Liz had found the Borkholder family. They'd quickly become special to her and a cherished link to her mother. Through them she had learned about her mom's Amish childhood and was led to a new place in the world with family and good friends.

The inn had filled another hole in her life. It had given her people to care for, something she sorely missed after her son, Steve, left home. Technically, Steve was her godson, but she had become his mother when he was seven years old after his parents died in a car accident. A soldier deployed in Kosovo, Liz worried about him every day, but during one of their many video chats he wisely said, "Channel your worry into action. Then it'll be good for something." And so she did.

"Is that coffee you've got there?" Mr. Hastings called out, waving at Liz.

"It is. So what are your plans for today?" Liz asked as she refilled his cup with fresh, hot coffee and then tended to his wife's. The retired couple had been frequent guests at the inn before Liz took over. Upon learning the bed-and-breakfast had reopened, they'd promptly called to book a room as "returning regulars."

"I want to visit Main Street," Mrs. Hastings said. "It's been quite a while since Donald and I roamed the town. Between the local artists and the Amish products, I intend to shop my heart out."

"While emptying out my wallet," Mr. Hastings added with a twinkle in his eye.

Liz hid a smile. Even when Mr. Hastings tried to grumble, he revealed how much he adored his wife.

Mrs. Hastings ignored her husband's comment. "I'm so glad the weather's cleared up. The rain would have put a crimp in my plans."

The month of May had roared in wet and windy, producing a steady succession of dark clouds and showers. But this dawn had come with plenty of sunshine, and the weather forecast promised it would be nice all day.

"Tell me, Liz, is Soap and Such still open?" Mrs. Hastings asked. "I bought some handmade lotions there years ago and would love to restock."

"It's still there in the very same spot on Main Street."

"Pleasant Creek is so charming." Mrs. Hastings looked out the window. "I almost forgot how quaint it is with the horse and buggies passing by."

Liz agreed. She, too, had been charmed by the downtown square with its large clock tower and flower beds. Old-fashioned gas lamps lined the streets, supporting hanging flower baskets bursting with color. The nearby Amish community had a presence in the town as well, evidenced by the hitching posts in the parking lots. The first time Liz had driven into town, the yellow caution sign featuring a horse and buggy had stumped her, until she realized it was to warn motorists to watch out for the Amish mode of travel.

"I must say, dear," Mrs. Hasting went on, "you've done wonders with this place since taking over the inn."

"Thank you." Liz smiled. "I'm so glad you think so."

"We've enjoyed sleeping in the Somewhere in Time Room. All those clocks! Donald loves it."

"Mmhm. I do," he mumbled around a mouthful of cinnamon bread.

Liz chuckled.

Taking ownership of the inn had been a major learning experience. The kitchen was already state of the art, but the guest rooms and common areas had needed updating. Her favorite room in the mansion was the library. She'd been enthralled by the collection of old instruments displayed in one of the floor-to-ceiling bookshelves—a clarinet, a flute, a recorder, an entire shelf of harmonicas, and even a few kazoos thrown into the mix. She'd wondered why the previous owners left them behind, but she was glad they did. Liz left the collection in place, and they never failed to spark a conversation.

"I'm thrilled to see Sew Welcome still on the premises." Mrs. Hastings nodded toward the sewing shop.

Liz smiled. The owners of Sew Welcome had definitely made themselves . . . so very welcome.

When Liz first moved in, two friendly women had arrived on her doorstep—uninvited. Liz had been completely floored when they announced their intention to take over two empty rooms on the inn's first floor and use them for their fabric shop. Liz soon learned that the women had been leasing the space for decades, vacating only recently because the inn had closed.

Before Liz knew what was what, Mary Ann Berne and Sadie Schwarzentruber barged into her life with their overflowing boxes of fabric, trailed by the three other members of the Material Girls quilting club. Between the forces of energy these five women created and the scrumptious pie Mary Ann had enticed Liz with, she'd lost the battle before it began. In fact, she happily became a Material Girl herself and made dear friends of each of the other women in record time.

"Do you quilt, Mrs. Hastings?" Liz asked.

"I took a class once here—at Sew Welcome. Made a beautiful wall hanging."

"Yes," Mr. Hastings added, "a class that was supposed to be fifty dollars ended up costing me a hundred."

"You'll never let me live that down, will you?"

The older man cracked a smile. "Never."

Liz understood. Aside from offering lessons in everything from basic stitching to advanced quilt making, Sew Welcome was a cornucopia of tempting sewing supplies. It was nearly impossible not to overbuy.

After patting Mr. Hastings on the shoulder, Liz placed the carafe on the sideboard, scanning the length of it to see if any dishes needed to be refilled. Satisfied there was enough food and that everything was under control, she decided to take a few minutes to pop into Sew Welcome. Maybe someone in the shop had seen her missing dog this morning.

Mary Ann greeted Liz as she stepped through the door. Mary Ann, a talented quilter in her early sixties with a stylish silver bob, was as kindhearted as she was take-charge. After seeing her in action, Liz understood why the fabric shop was such a hit with locals and tourists.

"Looks like your guests are enjoying breakfast this morning," Mary Ann commented from behind the counter in the showroom.

"They are. Especially Mr. Hastings." Liz crossed the room. "Interest in the inn has been steady."

"That's good news. As word gets out, you can expect full weekends."

"A lot of thanks goes to you for that."

Mary Ann and Sadie had contributed to the inn's successful reopening. Whenever they had customers who were traveling over an hour for quilting classes, her friends never failed to recommend that they stay the night.

Mary Ann tucked a strand of sleek, silver hair behind her ear. "So why are you here instead of pampering your guests?"

"I was wondering if you've seen Beans this morning."

"No, I can't say that I have."

Liz frowned. "It's not like him to be gone so long. Or to miss breakfast."

"I wouldn't worry. Most likely something caught his attention outside."

"That's what I'm afraid of. He doesn't usually go near the lake, but what if he decided to chase after a squirrel and fell in?"

"Knowing Beans, I doubt he ran after anything. He'll be back when he's hungry."

"Most days he barely gets off his rug," Liz said, voicing her concerns to her level-headed friend.

"Don't worry until there's something to worry about." Mary Ann strode to one of the shelves and beckoned Liz to follow. "Sadie asked me to show you the new fabric she ordered. She claims it's perfect for your project."

Since coming to Pleasant Creek, Liz had started quilting again. Her late mother had taught her when she was young, one of many beautiful memories she had of her mother. During college and law school, however, there'd been no free time for the craft. Then, after school, a busy career took precedence. After Liz became Steve's guardian, it seemed as if she barely had time to sleep, much less quilt. To her delight, she'd picked it right up again, only being a bit rusty with a needle at first.

The fabric that Mary Ann showed Liz was a soft shade of blue with a small geometric design and, as Sadie had claimed, was perfect for Liz's new bedspread project. Liz hadn't spent nearly enough time making her private quarters in the inn feel like home, and she hoped the new spread would brighten up her bedroom.

"Sadie's a genius." Liz ran her hand across the fabric. At seventy years old and sporting the nickname "Crazy Quilter," Sadie had more energy than a lot of women half her age. She was also one of the most gifted quilters Liz had ever met.

"I agree," Mary Ann said, "but let's keep that between us. Sadie already lets us know just how wonderful she is. We don't want to give her more encouragement."

Liz chuckled. Sadie definitely spoke her mind.

Before she had a chance to discuss the fabric choice further, Sarah poked her head into the doorway. "We need more muffins."

"On it." Liz smiled at Mary Ann. "Duty calls. We'll chat later."

"Count on it. And don't worry about Beans. He'll be home when he's ready."

Home. Liz loved the sound of it.

"Oh, and Liz? Will you be joining us for the meeting tonight? Opal and Caitlyn will be here for sure. And Naomi plans to stop by after she closes the bakery. We're deciding on our next group project."

The Material Girls were a diverse yet tightly knit group of stitchers. Opal was a reserved older woman who doted on her husband, George. Caitlyn was a fun-loving girl in her twenties who worked at the hospital. And Naomi was close to Liz's age and owned a bakery in town.

When she'd lived in Boston, Liz had too many excuses not to meet her friends, first and foremost being busy with work and raising her godson. She had only socialized occasionally. Now, as a resident of Pleasant Creek, she always made time for her new friends. And since her love for quilting had returned, she made sure she fit time to sew into her day.

"It should be a quiet evening at the inn. I don't see any reason why I can't make it. Besides, now that I've seen the fabric Sadie ordered, I'm ready to get busy cutting out pieces for the new quilt top."

"Great. We'll see you later."

The next hour passed in a blur. Liz chatted with her guests and directed them to different shops on Main Street. But by the time she and Sarah had the dishes washed and the kitchen straightened out, their resident dog still hadn't woofed at the door to be let in.

"Okay, that's it." Pulling the apron over her head, Liz hung it on a hook by the pantry. "I'm going out to hunt down Beans."

"I'll start cleaning the guest rooms." Sarah also removed her kitchen apron, knocking her *Kapp* slightly askew. Meticulously straightening the black headpiece that was indicative of her recent marriage, Sarah tucked a few strands of blond hair back inside the bonnet before donning a worn apron and gathering her cleaning items. "You know he will be fine, *ja*? He has gotten into mischief before."

"I believe you, but until I see him for myself, I'm going to worry." Liz only hoped her search didn't turn into a rescue.

"Rub his belly for me when you find him," Sarah called as she left the kitchen.

"Right after I have a few choice words with him for throwing off my morning," Liz muttered.

Ready to embark on her mission, Liz opened the utility-room door, took one step, and promptly tripped over something sprawled in the doorway.

2

Liz stumbled outside, managing to jump over the dog and then right herself, just saving herself from landing face first on the concrete. Beans dropped whatever had been in his mouth and gave a loud woof in greeting.

"*Beans!* Where have you been?" Liz put her hands on her hips and tried to look stern, but his innocent eyes and happy face made her smile.

"Don't give me that look. I've been worried." She examined the dog to make sure he hadn't hurt himself. To her dismay, the plump bulldog had managed to turn himself a dingy color of brown. Days of spring rain had soaked the earth, and Beans had covered himself in a layer of mud. "And where have you been? You're filthy."

Beans wagged his stubby tail in response.

"Oh, you're happy about that?"

Beans wagged some more and broke into a wide, panting grin.

"Okay, you're still adorable, but there's no way you're going inside like that, mister. C'mon."

Beans followed Liz to the water spigot at the back of the inn. She grabbed the hose, turned on the water, and proceeded to rinse off her mud-encrusted pet.

Beans gave her a look of disappointment as if she'd betrayed him.

"You started it," she said. "Plus, everyone loves a clean dog. You'll get lots of pets today."

He barked once and then tried to lick at the spray of water.

Liz laughed and let him get a drink from the hose while she checked to see that all of the mud was rinsed off. Stepping back to admire her work, she said, "Now, that wasn't so bad, was it?"

The dog shook himself, sending water flying everywhere, including all over Liz. "One good turn deserves another, I guess." She wiped the water off her arms.

Beans trotted alongside Liz to the back entrance of the inn. At the door, he picked up the object that had fallen out of his mouth.

"Oh, I see. You went digging and found something." Liz leaned down to take a closer look. She reached out to take the item from him, but Beans turned his head, not about to let her take his prize.

Liz tilted her head and studied the object as best she could. It looked like Beans had an old, brown bone in his mouth.

"Oh, yuck. Where did you get that?"

Beans shifted the bone in his mouth, and Liz got a better look at it. Dread washed over her. Her palms grew clammy and a prickling fluttered over the back of her neck.

Liz's gut told her that it wasn't a bone from last night's steak. *It can't be.*

But it definitely looked like . . . a human bone.

"Oh Beans."

Beans gave Liz an innocent look, turned, and trotted down the steps. Liz followed. He stopped at a small pile in the yard and dropped his new toy. Swallowing hard, she crouched down to see what Beans had collected.

Liz sank to the grass. "This is not good."

If she guessed correctly, he'd amassed a collection of finger bones. Human finger bones.

Beans laid beside her and barked, as if agreeing with her assessment.

Once she got her wits about her, Liz rolled to her knees. She rubbed Beans's head, took a bracing breath, and moved closer to the bones.

An otherworldly kind of curiosity gripped her.

Sure enough, nestled in the slender blades of grass were different-size brown bones. They were in bad shape, as if they'd been buried in the ground for a long while, degraded from exposure to the earth and elements.

"Why couldn't you have brought me a stick?" Liz asked Beans, whose ears perked up to let Liz know that he was listening. "That's what normal dogs do. Now what am I to do?"

Liz stood up, her mind racing. *I should call the police. Definitely call the police.* Yet her feet remained rooted to the ground even as her knees wobbled.

"Li-iz," a female voice spoke in singsong. "Oh, Liz?"

Hearing the high-pitched voice summon her, Liz's head shot up. To her dismay, Mrs. Hastings, outfitted in her electric-pink jogging suit and pristine white sneakers, power-walked directly toward her, which would have been fine if there weren't what she suspected to be human remains lying in the grass less than a foot away.

Liz took a few big steps forward and tried to sound unconcerned. "Mrs. Hastings. What can I do for you?"

"My husband has decided to stay behind and read a book in your lovely four-season room." The woman sniffed. "The bowl of toffees on the table beside his chair isn't giving him incentive to move either."

"That's a problem?"

"Of course. He fusses about my shopping, but I must admit, woman to woman, he's a keen bargain hunter. He can nose out a buried treasure like no one I've ever met."

Liz glanced over her shoulder. Not that she considered human bones a "treasure," but she didn't want any of her guests learning about what Beans had unearthed until she'd had a chance to notify the police.

Mrs. Hastings craned her neck to see around Liz. "Is something wrong?"

Pasting on a smile, Liz guided her guest back toward the inn. "Oh, no. Beans just decided it was a time for a spa day. He took a mud bath, which meant I had to give him a shower."

Beans rose on plump legs as if defending himself. After a testy woof, he loped after them toward the utility room door.

"He likes to pretend he's lazy, but don't let him fool you." Mrs. Hastings lowered her voice to a whisper as if Beans might hear her. "That pooch is always into something."

"Usually a bowl of food," Liz said as she led Mrs. Hastings and Beans into the kitchen.

Beans waddled to his kibble and tucked in to his breakfast, his ghastly discovery officially turned over to Liz.

She sighed. *Thanks a lot, Beans.*

"How can I convince my husband to join me?" Mrs. Hasting's voice jolted Liz from her thoughts.

Liz lowered her voice and leaned toward her guest. "I think all you have to do is ask him nicely. He clearly adores you."

Mrs. Hastings beamed. "He does, doesn't he?"

"I'm sure he'll be happy to give up his book in favor of treasure hunting."

"You know, dear, you could have a career as a counselor of some sort."

Liz chuckled. "You don't need counseling. I think you two could give seminars on how to have a happy marriage."

Glowing with excitement, Mrs. Hastings set off as Liz washed her arms from fingertips to elbows, her mind returning to the bones in her yard. After she dried off, she grabbed her cell phone off the counter, started to call the police department, but then stopped. Knowing Beans, he hadn't traveled off the property. Today's events were highly out of character for the normally lethargic dog, which meant he'd probably dug up the bones somewhere on the grounds. And if, in fact, he *did* find them on the inn's property, Liz might have an even bigger problem on her hands. Namely, an inn filled with guests who might very well stumble upon the same gruesome discovery!

She pulled open a cabinet drawer of kitchen towels. Taking an older one, she went back outside and headed straight to the pile of bones. She placed the towel loosely over the bones, pressing the edges into the grass to keep it from moving in the breeze.

After securing the towel, she made her way along the perimeter of the house. Her feet sank into the still dew-soaked grass as she walked the perimeter, hoping Beans hadn't created too big of a mess. The red brick of the inn gleamed in the morning sunlight, yet she couldn't find one place where the ground had been disturbed. She made her way around to the front of the inn just as Sadie sauntered up the sidewalk.

"Good morning, Liz. Lovely day."

"Hmm?" Liz glanced up. "Oh yes. Lovely."

Wearing a floppy, navy-blue hat adorned with white pompoms along the edge and carrying a large tote bag that was most likely holding her current quilting project, Sadie stopped beside Liz. "Did you lose something?"

"More like found something."

"Go on then."

Liz looked up to meet shrewd blue eyes. "I . . . Beans found something."

"Dogs do that, dear."

If you only knew, Sadie.

"Did you get a chance to look at the fabric I picked out for you?" Sadie asked.

Liz shaded her eyes against the bright sun as she scanned the yard. "Yes, Mary Ann showed me."

"I knew you'd love the pink."

"It's great." *Why couldn't Beans at least leave a trail for me?*

"And the purple pattern? Perfect for your green bedroom."

"Just what I'd hoped for," Liz said absently, checking the profusion of pink peonies planted beside the steps leading up to the front porch. She'd intended the flowers to greet her guests as they came up the front walk, but now she wondered if they concealed something more sinister.

"The fabric is blue." Sadie blew out an exasperated breath. "Are you listening to me?"

"What? Sorry. I'm trying to find where Beans dug up his, um, prize."

"I can see this is important. Don't let me keep you." Sadie waved a hand and continued up the sidewalk before stopping abruptly. "By the way, have you spoken to Miriam?"

At the mention of Miriam's name, Liz halted her search and made eye contact with Sadie. "Not lately. Is she okay?"

Although Liz had come to find out she was related to Miriam Borkholder, her Amish cousin, they didn't talk on a daily basis. Miriam had enough on her plate with six children at home to raise, a house to take care of, and quilting lessons to teach.

"Yes, she's fine. We have her scheduled to teach a class at Sew Welcome. She has a delightful treadle sewing machine she's going to leave at the shop for demonstrations. Your guests might enjoy learning some of her Amish quilting techniques."

Always eager to find ways to keep guests engaged at the inn, Liz was all for the idea. It also meant more time to visit with Miriam who had become as close as a sister to Liz. "I'll swing by the shop later."

Sadie nodded, and her hat flapped in agreement. "Carry on."

Liz continued her quest around the house, all the way back to square one. *Nothing.*

She blew out a breath and looked toward Jaynes Lake, located behind the inn. *Maybe Beans found the bones there?* At a slight jog, Liz hurried across the yard to the water's edge. Finding nothing unusual or out of place, she tamped down her frustration.

As she turned to make her way back to the house, out of the corner of her eye Liz glimpsed a familiar bench. Positioned on the side of the property, it was almost completely surrounded by lilac bushes. She walked there as if on autopilot. Since buying the inn and moving to Pleasant Creek, this had become her favorite place to sit outside. Featuring a panoramic view of the lake and surrounding grounds, Liz could unwind and reflect on the day's events, ponder what she had in store for the week ahead, or lose herself in a good book. The lilacs were a beautiful springtime bonus in this place she'd come to think of as her sanctuary.

The sweet scent of the abundant pale bluish-purple blossoms reached her nose as she drew closer. Bees hovered, bobbing from one flower to the next. When she'd first moved in, the inn's grounds had been in sorry shape. With her other part-time employee, sixteen-year-old Kiera Williams, Liz had worked on sprucing up the yard. And to her great joy, the lovely bushes had come back to life.

Approaching the bench, she noticed clumps of dirt littering the surrounding grass. A trail, she realized, rounded the bench. Sure enough, beside one of the bushes, the earth had been disrupted.

With a small cry of dismay, Liz knelt beside the lilac bush. The bright sun caused her to squint, but she noticed an object with a blue edge sticking out of the soil. Gingerly brushing the dirt aside, she exposed the edge of a piece of plastic.

She sank back on her heels in confusion. "A plastic bag?"

Relieved that her discovery didn't include any other bones, she tugged the plastic with one hand, scooping away the dirt around the edges with her other. The small bag finally came loose, and Liz pulled it free. She dusted the remaining debris from the clear protective covering to get a better look.

The bag held a photo and a folded piece of paper. The photograph looked like a sepia-toned print from a tourist attraction where people dressed up in period clothing and posed for the camera. On closer inspection, Liz realized it *was* a truly old print. The image looked a bit blurry, and the edges were worn as if it had been handled a great many times.

The couple in the picture displayed a serious, stately air. From the style of their clothing, she guessed it was taken in the late 1800s. The young woman wore a high-collared dress, her hair severely pulled back and her hands tightly clasped in her lap. Her expression gave away nothing. The gentleman, his hair slicked back, sported a dapper mustache. He rested a hand on the seated woman's shoulder. In his eyes, however, Liz detected a bit of a twinkle. Despite their stiff postures, a sense of happiness radiated from the couple.

She turned the bag over to view the yellowed paper. A few words of handwriting were revealed. The salutation was clear: *All my love, Emma.*

Liz traced a finger over the image. *Emma? Emma who?*

"Ms. Eckardt?" Sarah's voice made her jump.

Liz turned in the girl's direction.

"I have finished upstairs. Do you need anything else?"

"No thanks, Sarah. You're finished for the day."

The young Amish woman stopped before Liz, her gray dress immaculate even after cleaning the inn.

"You look upset," Sarah said. "Is something wrong?"

Liz held up the bag. "I'm not entirely sure."

Sarah stepped closer. "What is it?"

"A photograph and a letter." *And bones.* Liz didn't mention the other discovery for fear of upsetting Sarah.

"From where?"

Liz looked back at the ground. "Buried in the dirt. Beans must have unearthed this when he dug around the lilac bush this morning."

"Do you know who it belongs to?"

"That's the question of the hour."

Sarah shrugged. "I must get home."

"Sure. I'll see you tomorrow."

"Yes. And I will bring *Mutter's* sourdough starter and recipe like I promised."

"Sounds great." Liz wanted to serve some Amish treats as a way of incorporating her heritage into the food choices at the inn, so she was always on the lookout for new recipes.

Sarah started back to the house, but Liz stopped her. "Please don't say anything about what I found to anyone. At least not until I figure out what I have here."

By the disinterest reflected on the girl's face, Liz suspected she'd already moved on to the usual things young women thought about.

Although in Sarah's case, she was probably thinking about her new husband, Isaac Borkholder, Miriam's oldest son. Sarah most likely had her mind on her home, not the contents of Liz's plastic bag.

With a nod, Sarah bade, *"Auf wiedersen."*

"That's supposing I can make any sense out of what I've found," Liz whispered to herself after she returned the nod.

Liz turned to face the bush again. Gently laying the plastic bag on the bench, she took a deep breath. The late morning sun beat against her neck. She brushed a strand of hair from her eyes, all the while focusing on the area of earth Beans had disrupted.

Do I dare keep digging?

Once she called the police, they would more than likely cordon off the area to determine if there were any other remains. Then they would take the evidence, and the news would leak out. Liz knew well enough from her criminal law class not to muck around with a possible crime scene.

Deciding not to disturb the ground any further, Liz picked up the bag and headed back to the house to call the authorities. Her mind intent on the contents of the bag as she went, she stepped on something hard and her ankle turned. Completely losing her balance, she teetered and fell to the grass, eyes wide at the object beside her foot.

Another bone.

3

Within an hour the police were camped out on Liz's property. The low murmur of concerned voices carried over the quiet backyard, an eerie contrast to a bird cheerfully singing in the distance. Arms wrapped around her middle, Liz stood on the sidelines, hopelessly watching her beloved lilac bushes become collateral damage as the officers dug for more remains.

One of the policemen took a large evidence bag, weighed down with what she assumed were newly discovered skeletal remains, to a van parked in her gravel parking lot. Another officer continued taking photographs of the site. The ground surrounding her favorite bench had been cordoned off with yellow tape so no one could disturb the scene. Thankfully, the guests were still out exploring the town. But knowing Pleasant Creek, word would spread quickly and she'd have some explaining to do before long.

For now, Liz stood alone halfway between the crime scene and the inn wondering where the bones had come from. Beans, the traitor, had ignored the commotion and opted for a nap.

A stocky, gray-haired man that Liz had come to know rather well approached her. "We've gotten everything we need."

She lifted a brow at Stan Houghton, Pleasant Creek's chief of police. "Which is?"

"Human remains, but I think you already knew that."

She nodded, her throat suddenly feeling dry as a bone.

"I'm not an expert," the chief continued, "but I'd say whoever that is, they've been in the ground a long time. Along with retrieving the rest of the evidence, we took soil samples. Although, judging from the age of the remains, I'm not sure if we'll find any answers."

"I guess that's good for me. Leaves me out of the running as a suspect." She attempted a smile.

"We never suspected you, Liz."

"Thanks for the vote of confidence, Chief."

His words went a long way in calming her queasy stomach. Stan Houghton might be a very amiable man on first meeting, but she would never question his sharp intellect.

"What about the plastic bag I found in the area where Beans was digging?"

The chief held up another clear evidence bag with the smaller bag inside and examined it. "The contents are old, but the bag is new. Not weathered like you'd expect if it had been buried in the dirt for any length of time. Hard to tell if there's a connection. I'll need to take it to the station."

"Of course. And the bones? I guess they'll be sent out to be analyzed?"

Chief Houghton nodded. "I'm not sure if we'll get any DNA, let alone a hit that tells us who it is."

"Is that because the bones are, er, might be old?"

"That's right. But for now, this as a crime scene. You know the drill."

Yes, she did. Liz hadn't practiced criminal law, but she knew what to expect at a crime scene. It was one of the many reasons finding the bones on her property had her in knots.

"Do you think they've always been buried here or were they moved?" Liz asked.

"That's one of the questions I'm hoping to answer."

Liz exhaled, realizing she'd been holding her breath.

The chief placed a firm hand on her shoulder. "You've had quite a shock today."

The chief's kindness pulled Liz back to more immediate concerns. "What do I tell my guests?"

"The truth, I expect. Look, the findings appear old. It's not like the scene is recent, except for the plastic bag you found under the bush."

"Having all of this evidence discovered on my property just feels so . . . personal."

"I understand. As soon as we learn anything, I'll let you know. Meantime, try not to dwell on it."

As if that's an option. Shivering, despite standing in the warm glow of the sun, Liz wondered about the couple in the photo. Why had someone gone to the trouble of leaving those particular items on her property?

Liz pointed to the bag of evidence. "Any chance I can get photocopies of the picture and letter?"

The chief nodded. "Gimme a few days."

"You know I'm going to hold you to that." Liz was nothing if not tenacious, and her lawyer's mind was already in high gear.

Tipping his hat, the chief cracked a smile. "Sure do."

As she walked back inside the inn, Liz decided she'd find out more about the woman who signed the letter. *Emma.* Maybe that information would shed light on who had left the bag. She'd barely made it into the kitchen when Mary Ann and Sadie intercepted her.

"I'm so glad you finally came inside," Mary Ann said. "We saw the police cars pull up and couldn't imagine what was wrong."

Sadie nodded. "I wanted to march right out there and ask Chief Houghton what was going on, but Mary Ann stopped me."

"You have to let the man do his job."

Sadie shrugged. "I know, but I want answers."

"Which I told you we'd get when Liz came in." Mary Ann's worried gaze met Liz's. "We saw you talking to the chief but didn't want to interfere."

Liz could only stare at her. *Really? Since when?*

"We've been worried sick about you," Sadie insisted, an expectant look on her face.

Liz figured she must have a shell-shocked expression on her own face because Sadie dragged her into the sitting room and pushed her into a comfy armchair.

"You look like you've seen a ghost, my dear."

Liz shivered. "Not quite, but close."

"I'm going to fix us all some tea," Mary Ann announced. "Do *not* say anything until I get back."

Sadie took a seat on the armrest of Liz's chair. "Are you okay?"

Liz brushed her hair from her forehead. "Yes. It's not as bad as I imagine the two of you have made it out to be."

"Well, we had to wait until we could talk to you to learn any details. Until then, we played the speculation game."

"Which is probably nowhere near the truth."

"It never is."

Ten minutes later Mary Ann came back carrying a tray loaded down with a teapot and cups. Liz took the offered cup. "It all began—"

Mary Ann held up a hand to stop her. "Perhaps we should wait for Opal and Caitlyn."

Liz blinked. "How would they know about—"

"Oh, please. You don't think news of the police crawling all over your property hasn't spread around town? Along with the fact that they were seen digging up your yard?" Mary Ann chuckled. "The girls called here within five minutes of each other."

After taking a sip of tea, Liz rested her head back and closed her eyes. The adrenaline of finding the remains had begun to wear off. Her limbs felt heavy, and she had to shake off the lethargy descending upon her.

A ruckus sounded in the foyer. Liz's eyes shot open as Naomi rushed into the room. Her shoulder-length dark hair was pulled back, her brown eyes wide.

Naomi knelt beside Liz. "Please tell me you're okay." Still dressed in her work clothes, she smelled sweet, like the bakery she'd just left.

Knowing her friends were there for her was a huge relief to Liz. "I'm fine. The police weren't here because anything happened to me."

Naomi placed her hand over her heart. "Oh, thank goodness. When I heard . . . my mind went haywire."

"No need to overreact, dear," Sadie spoke up. "Mary Ann and I were here the entire time."

"This better be good," Caitlyn announced as she entered the room. "I just got off from my overnight shift at the hospital, and I feel like the walking dead."

Liz felt herself wince at the reference.

"And I left George at home to fend for himself," Opal chimed in as she trailed Caitlyn. "He'll probably end up going to Mama's Home Cooking for lunch."

When the women settled in, five sets of eyes focused on Liz. It was time to tell the story of the events of the morning. She set her cup on the coffee table. "It all started when I let Beans out this morning."

She explained the muddy dog's adventure, resulting in the discovery of bones beneath the lilac bush.

"That explains why you were so absentminded when I spoke to you earlier," Sadie said. "You were looking for the spot where Beans found the bones." Liz nodded. "I was so freaked out. I had to find where he dug them up before someone else did. After Beans showed me the pile of bones he'd collected, I guess he figured his job was over. He ate and fell asleep."

"Any idea who the bones belong to?" Caitlyn asked, her red-streaked hair a contrast to the powder-blue scrubs she wore.

"No. They have to be sent off to a lab and analyzed."

Naomi shuddered.

Liz continued, "The odd thing is, they appear to be really old."

Sadie frowned. "I don't recall there being a burial site on the inn's property. Do you, Mary Ann?"

"The town cemetery has been used for generations as far as I know."

"There's no guarantee that testing will even determine whose remains they are," Liz said.

"How very odd," Sadie murmured.

"Oh, that's not the strangest part," Liz continued. "After I located the spot where Beans had found the bones, I came across a plastic bag. Inside it was an old photo and a letter signed by someone named Emma."

The women in the room exchanged curious glances.

"What type of photo?" Opal finally asked.

"An old-fashioned type of print featuring a couple. The style of clothing looked to be from more than a century ago. They both had serious expressions on their faces."

"Do you still have it?"

"The chief took it." Liz waved a hand. "I know it's evidence, but I hated letting go of it."

"Why is that?" Sadie asked.

"I guess since I found it on my property. I know it's not mine, but after seeing the photo and letter, I couldn't help but wonder about the couple. Is the letter important? Why doesn't the family have it?" Liz stopped and shook her head. "I know it's silly, but I'm hooked now. I want to know more."

Naomi leaned forward in her seat. "Okay. So now what?"

"First, I assure my guests there's nothing to worry about. There's no murderer running loose around town burying bones—at least not in this century."

"And the picture?" Sadie asked.

"I do have an idea."

Naomi cleared her throat. "Oh boy. I've seen that look on your face before, and I know what it means."

Liz grinned. "It means I'm going to get to the bottom of who left that plastic bag in my dirt and why."

Opal looked worried. "Isn't that what the police are supposed to do?"

"I'm sure they wouldn't mind a little help. Besides, this is a crime to them. To me . . . it's personal. I have to know why someone would leave the bag with its contents on my property and whether or not it's connected to those bones. I want to know the story behind the couple in the photo."

"Cool." Caitlyn scooted to the edge of her seat. "What do you have in mind?"

"Right now, not much. Chief Houghton is going to let me have a copy of the photo and the letter. Once I read the entire letter, maybe I'll have a better idea what to look for."

"You know," Opal said, her eyes bright as she spoke, "I'm a member of the local Women in History chapter. You've heard me talk about it."

"You do genealogies and stuff like that?" Caitlyn asked.

"Precisely. We meet once a month and put on fundraisers a few times a year."

"How could they help?" Liz asked.

"One of our members, our president in fact, is a renowned historian with a doctorate in her field. Her name is Althea Mitchell. She's a genealogy expert, and she's currently writing a paper on her ancestors and their roles in the Civil War."

Liz felt a jolt of excitement. "Do you think she'd be willing to look at the photo and letter when I get my copies?"

"Althea is always very busy, so I can't make any promises, but I bet she'll be as intrigued as we are. Once you have the photo and letter, I'll make an appointment for us to see her."

Caitlyn, always up for an adventure, grinned. "This is getting good already."

"Then it's settled. We'll look into the mysterious couple and try to figure out why someone would leave a photo of them in my backyard."

The women rose, chatting and collecting teacups to carry into the kitchen. Once they'd said their goodbyes, Liz stood at the kitchen window, her gaze drawn to the crime scene. Yellow perimeter tape fluttered in the breeze.

"You know," came Mary Ann's voice behind her, "you're undertaking a big project. I don't want you to be disappointed if no information comes your way."

Liz turned. "I've always been curious. My mother told me it would get me into trouble one day, but it made me a good lawyer."

"An inquisitive lawyer and a curious innkeeper are two different things."

Liz shrugged. "Doesn't mean I'm going to change."

Mary Ann sighed. "Can I give you one word of caution?"

"Sure."

"The bones are unpleasant, but the fact that someone left that photo and letter is downright suspicious. You might be getting involved in something you have no business sticking your nose into."

"Then whoever left that plastic bag should have put it in someone else's yard."

Mary Ann nodded. "Please be careful."

"I will. Don't worry about me."

"I can't help it. You're a Material Girl. We watch out for each other. And now that you've gotten us all interested in finding out the story behind the couple . . ."

"You included?"

"Of course. I like to be the voice of reason in our group, but I'm still in."

Liz laughed out loud. No way could Mary Ann keep from sticking her nose into the mystery in Liz's backyard. "Good to know."

Mary Ann patted Liz's arm. "I have to get back to the shop."

As her friend left, Liz turned to stare out the window, rubbing her arms against the chill that had invaded her kitchen. She couldn't stop thinking about the woman in the photo. *Who are you, Emma? And do you know anything about the bones in my yard?*

4

Before Liz had to face her returning guests, she had time for her weekly video chat with her godson, Steve, who was stationed in Kosovo. He expressed concern for her safety when she told him about the bones, but Liz assured him she would be fine and that the chief would find out who the remains belonged to. As for her part, she would only try to learn more about Emma, which shouldn't lead to any danger—right? Steve knew better than to try to talk his godmother out of pursuing the matter, so instead, he made Liz promise to keep her guard up and not take unnecessary risks.

After she signed off, Liz brewed fresh coffee and set out a plate of chocolate chip cookies for the customary late afternoon snack. The cookies were a good choice because Liz needed an infusion of chocolate to get through the next hurdle of her day—explaining to her guests why police tape had suddenly appeared in place of lilac bushes.

Mr. and Mrs. Hastings, along with a retired administrative assistant and a cross-country traveling couple, cornered her in the sitting room.

As everyone spoke at once, Liz held up her hand. "Please, everyone remain calm. I can assure you there's no danger. The police have the matter taken care of. The . . . findings don't appear to be new, so there is no reason to believe anyone is out to hurt any of us."

"How can you be so sure? So calm?" Mrs. Hastings snatched up a magazine from the coffee table and fanned herself.

"I trust the police."

"I'm afraid I can't stay," the assistant said, her voice shaky. "I'll go get my things."

Liz's heart sank as she watched the woman leave. What toll would Beans's discovery take on her business?

"How do you know there aren't more remains somewhere on the property?" Mrs. Hastings asked in hushed voice, as if speaking quietly would keep any more bad news at bay.

"Edna," her husband said, "no need to make the situation any worse. I'm sure Liz has everything well in hand."

Actually, wrapping her mind around one discovery was enough, but what if there *were* more bones waiting to be found? No, Liz didn't want to think about it. She turned to address the small crowd. "I'm sorry this has happened. If you want to check out now, I'll understand."

The traveling couple declined and retreated back to the Amish Room.

Liz faced Mr. And Mrs. Hastings. "If you're that upset—"

"Liz, we won't leave you in your time of need, will we, Donald?"

"Not unless she wants us to."

"Of course I don't," Liz rushed to say.

"We insist on staying until we find out just what is going on."

We? "I appreciate your support, but there's no telling how long this case will take the police to figure out—if they get anywhere on it at all, that is."

"It's settled." Mrs. Hastings spoke as if she hadn't heard Liz. "We're staying a few more days at least. Tell her, Donald."

Mr. Hastings winked at Liz. "Whatever my wife wants."

It took two days before Liz's curiosity got the better of her. Chief Houghton hadn't gotten back to her, so she decided to visit the station after serving breakfast to her remaining guests. Forced to change because of an unfortunate coffee splatter, Liz dressed up a bit in a pale yellow short-sleeved blouse, denim skirt, and flat sandals. After running a brush through her hair, she grabbed her purse, told Sarah she was leaving, and walked into town.

Another glorious day had dawned over Pleasant Creek. The

sun shone brightly in the cobalt sky. Birds sang as she passed under the shade of tall maple trees. A slow-moving open buggy, drawn by a cinnamon-color horse, lumbered by. Liz smiled at the occupants. Everything was as it should be on an idyllic late-spring day, except for the questions circling in her mind.

Those questions had been popping up with regular frequency. Liz was eager to read the letter and find out to whom Emma was sending her love. Perhaps learning more about the mystery woman would set the entire situation to rights.

If only life were that easy.

The police station was housed in a nondescript brick building. Liz entered the foyer, instantly chilled by the air-conditioned gusts blasting through the space. The uniformed officer assigned to desk duty greeted her and asked for her name. Before she had a chance to explain why she'd stopped by, the eager young man picked up the receiver from the phone on his desk.

"Chief? You have company." He replaced the handset. "The chief will be right out, Ms. Eckardt."

"I take it you were expecting me?"

The man shrugged and busied himself with the computer on his desk, but Liz didn't miss the amused expression that crossed his face.

A door near the back of the building opened. The chief strode toward her, his face expressionless. "You do know we are investigating the matter," he said by way of greeting.

"And I'm certain you are doing a very thorough job of it. I just want to find out more about the author of the letter."

The chief leaned into her space, a tactic she suspected was meant to discourage her quest.

"Look," he said, voice stern, but not enough to scare her off. "I understand the curiosity, but I don't know if throwing yourself into the investigation of an unknown person is wise."

"She's not unknown. Her name is Emma."

"Not much to go on."

"I'm sure you've launched an investigation with far less evidence."

"True, but it's my job."

Liz nodded. "You're right. It probably won't lead anywhere. But I might as well at least try."

The chief's face softened. "If it weren't for the letter being found in a plastic bag, I wouldn't be concerned. But someone went out of their way to keep the contents protected and place them on your property." He paused. "This isn't some sort of history project, you know."

"I understand that. But it won't keep me from making inquiries."

The stocky man sighed and ran a hand through his gray hair.

"If it makes you feel any better, I promise to call you if I run into any problems."

He eyed her closely. "Or danger?"

"Of course."

The chief rubbed the bridge of his nose. "Okay. Fine." He walked to a desk, picked up a folder, and returned to Liz. "For the record, I am advising you against this." Chief Houghton's astute gaze challenged her.

"Duly noted, on the record," Liz said as she took his offering. She decided not to stick around, just in case he changed his mind. Besides, now that she had a copy of the letter, her fingers nearly trembled in anticipation. Liz couldn't wait to read the contents. It felt like months, not days, since she'd discovered the plastic bag. Now, she had only one task in mind. She hurried to The Coffee Cup where she could read in peace.

The scent of rich brewing coffee permeated the shop. Liz took a deep breath as she walked in. She really needed a cup right now. Placing her order for a mocha latte, she gazed at her surroundings. Only a few customers loitered this late in the morning, reading the newspaper or swiping a tablet, which was good for her. The fewer folks Liz knew here, the better chance she could read the letter uninterrupted. She took her latte and settled in at a table in the corner.

First, she examined the photo. Lighter than the original, she was still able to make out the faces and setting of the couple. On closer inspection, Liz noticed some details she hadn't been able to study before.

A watch chain looped from the man's vest to a pocket. She could make out the top of the watch, as if it hadn't been situated properly. How many times had he taken it out to read the time of day? Had it been a family heirloom? A gift from his beloved?

On the neckline of the woman's dress, Liz saw a brooch. She couldn't quite make out the design, but there appeared to be some sort of flower painted on it. Later, when she got back to the inn, she'd dig out her magnifying glass.

Liz set aside the photo and picked up the copy of the letter. She felt her heart beat a little faster as she unfolded it. The letter itself had been weathered and worn when Liz found it. Although she hadn't been able to read much when she first found it, she could tell the ink had faded with time. The photocopier had produced a good rendering of the original letter. She noticed a date in the corner—*1866*. If memory served, that was shortly after the Civil War ended. The neat cursive was legible, but the words were penned closely together with ink blotted in more than a few places. Liz began to read.

My dearest F,

While your last letter was very welcome, I cannot help but feel it was very dangerous as well. Although we have been separated these long months, my love has remained true. My heart aches with missing you, even as circumstances keep us apart. I thought going back to my old life would be easy. What a foolish idea. Nothing is the same, especially me.

I have kept our secret, difficult as it is since I want to tell the world of our love. We both know our families would never understand, yet I dare to hope. Hope that some way, someday, we find our way to each other.

Liz flipped the paper to the other side, engrossed in the anguish of the author. The hint of danger and love lost caught and kindled her imagination.

Am I foolish to hope and to dream? If so, then count me among those fools who pursue matters of the heart. No matter that it can never come to fruition. I hold the notion of happiness close to my chest. Your keepsake is ever with me, in my possession at all times. It's a part of you I will always hold dear.

This will be my last letter to you. My life has not turned out as I planned. People have not been what they seemed. It is safer for you that I end all correspondence. So this one last time, know that I wished for a different life, a different outcome, with you.

Stay safe. Live your life. Fondly remember me.

All my love, Emma

Liz stared at the words, a million questions bombarding her. But there was no Emma to ask. If, by chance, the remains were Emma's, had she been in danger? The letter hinted as much. But from whom? Certainly not the mysterious "F." The heartfelt words conveyed love for this man, not fear.

But then, why didn't he have the letter? It was clearly addressed and written to him. Had Emma not sent it?

"Something has your attention."

The deep voice startled Liz. She looked up to find Jackson Cross, mayor of Pleasant Creek, smiling at her. Rugged and good-looking, Jackson's thick brown hair was cut short, his hazel eyes curious as he glanced at the paper she held. His brow, drawn in a question, had her holding the letter close to her chest.

"Good morning, Jackson. I suppose you heard about the findings at the inn."

"I'd have to be deaf not to." He nodded to the empty seat at her table. "Do you mind?"

"Not at all. Have a seat."

"So, what are you reading?"

"There were more than just remains found on my property." She slid the photo across the small bistro table toward him.

Jackson picked up the copy to study. After a few moments, he looked at Liz. "Handsome couple."

"I'm going to go out on a limb here. By any chance do you recognize them?"

Jackson's gaze moved back to the photo, then to her. "Sorry. No."

"Didn't think so. I'm going to show it to the girls at Sew Welcome. Maybe one of them can place the couple."

"It's a pretty old picture. I wouldn't get my hopes up."

Liz opened her mouth and then thought better of it. Jackson probably wouldn't understand her need to find out who Emma was. The chief certainly didn't. The Material Girls, however, would have just as many questions.

After a brief silence, Jackson asked, "How are you doing? I mean about the remains found on your property."

"I'll admit, when I found Beans's cache, I was more than a little shaken. Stunned, actually." Liz took a sip of her latte, gathering her thoughts. "But Chief Houghton has things under control."

"Yet you're looking into the evidence?"

"You heard that through the town grapevine too?"

"I can see for myself." He gestured to the folder. Then he grinned at her. "I also heard it through the grapevine."

Liz pressed her lips together.

"What can I say?" Jackson shrugged. "Comes with the job title."

Will I ever get used to the small-town gossip mill? "I have personal reasons."

"Oh, personal reasons." Jackson rubbed his chin. "If I recall, those usually get in the way of better judgment."

"Point taken," Liz said. "How about I look at it less from a personal point of view and more as a history buff? I've always been a fan of American history. Having access to something very old and a bit mysterious, I can't help but be nosy. So sue me."

Jackson chuckled. "Not my line of work."

"If you found something unusual on your property, wouldn't you want to check into it?"

"Depends what it was, but, yeah, I'm sure I would."

Liz grinned. "So indulge me."

"The chief told me the photo and a letter were found together in a bag." Jackson's gaze pierced hers. "I have to admit, that concerns me."

"Me too. It's odd, to say the least. But what if it was placed there for a reason?"

"Exactly. What kind of reason would be a good one?"

"I don't know. That's what I intend to find out. Opal told me about a historian she knows. I'm going to call and set up an appointment with the woman." Liz took a sip of her drink. "Maybe once she sees what I have, she might offer some insight."

"Or it could lead to a dead end."

"Maybe, but I'm a glass-half-full kind of person." *Why am I being warned away by everyone?*

The barista called Jackson's name.

"That's my cue." He glanced at the counter. "I've got to get back to work."

"City hall or the furniture company?"

Jackson didn't only serve as mayor; his family owned Cross Furniture, a company that built high-end wood furniture, and he was its president. "Both, actually. I have a meeting with the city manager now. This afternoon I'll head to the shop to oversee an order."

"Busy man."

"That I am." He pointed to the picture. "Good luck. Let me know if I can be of any help."

As Jackson walked out the door, she reread the letter. Clearly, Emma was sending F a warning. Liz wondered if the unknown man had taken the advice.

Gathering her belongings, Liz ended her precious first minutes with the letter. She had work to do at the inn. The next day's breakfast menu hadn't been settled yet. Sarah had brought her mother's recipe for sourdough bread as promised, and Liz had plans to tackle it.

On the walk back to the inn, Liz waved and greeted friends and neighbors. A group of Amish girls in pastel blue dresses and white bonnets passed by. Curiosity and concern were evident in their expressions likely because most of the town had heard about the discovery at the inn. Liz confidently strolled along as if she hadn't a care, although her thoughts never veered far from the mysterious Emma and the bones that Beans had uncovered on her property. This wasn't something she could just forget about. She had to get to the bottom of it. The nagging certainty that the bones and the contents of the bag were linked hadn't abated since reading the letter and neither had her resolve to unravel the mystery behind it all. If anything, it had intensified. Yes, Liz might not like what she found, but she would proceed anyway.

She stopped at the antique mailbox located by the front steps of the inn to gather the day's mail and then fanned herself with the envelopes as she crossed the front porch. Letting herself in the front door, the cool interior immediately soothed her. Sew Welcome was noticeably silent. Perhaps potential customers had decided to keep a wide berth of the shop, just like some of her guests had of the inn. Right now only Mr. and Mrs. Hastings remained. Liz thought it was mostly out of curiosity, but she'd take it. Once the mystery behind the skeletal remains was solved, she hoped the inn could get back to normal.

Stopping by the reception desk, Liz looked over the day's mail. Bills. Advertisements. Nothing urgent.

She went to the kitchen, her mind already on the next task at hand, tomorrow's breakfast. Dropping her purse on the counter, she grabbed the recipe card Sarah had brought to her the day before. Taking it to the kitchen island to assemble the ingredients she needed to make sourdough bread, Liz noticed a white envelope. Curious, she ripped it open and removed a single sheet of paper with three words printed on it: *Please help Emma.*

5

Her stomach churning, Liz flipped over the envelope, but it was blank. There was no address and no postmark. So it was hand-delivered. But by whom? Concerned, Liz yelled, "Sarah? Where are you?"

"Upstairs."

Liz raced out of the kitchen and started climbing the stairs to find the teen rushing out of the Amish suite, a dust cloth in her hand. "Is something wrong, Ms. Eckardt?"

"Did you notice anyone hanging around here who shouldn't be?"

Sarah wiped her hands on her apron. "I don't think so. Just the Hastingses, but they went out for lunch."

"There hasn't been anyone near the kitchen?"

Sarah shook her head. "Did I do something wrong?"

Liz noticed the nervous expression on Sarah's face. "Not at all. I found something odd on the kitchen island."

"There were people in and out of Sew Welcome all morning. Quite a few local ladies were chatting out front after shopping, but that is all I know."

Enough scaring the poor girl. Sarah didn't have the answers Liz needed. "Thank you, Sarah. Sorry if I worried you. Everything's fine."

Sarah eyed her and said slowly, "I still have Mr. and Mrs. Hastings' room to straighten up."

"Go ahead. I'll be downstairs."

Liz returned to the kitchen, her skin prickling with nerves. Anyone entering or exiting the inn could have left the note. Folding it in half, she walked to the fabric shop.

"Hi, Liz. Any luck getting a copy of the letter from the police chief?" Sadie asked from her position by the antique notion case.

"Yes. I've read it through a few times already."

"And?"

"And I don't know what to make of it." Liz glanced around the showroom. "Do you expect to see Opal this afternoon?"

"I doubt it. She came by this morning."

"Okay. I'll give her a call. I want to set up a meeting with her historian friend." She turned to leave.

Sadie stopped her. "Liz? You're a bit distracted. Again."

Liz tightened her grasp on the note in her hand. "Sorry. Just thinking."

"So, are you going to let us read the letter?"

"Yes. It's in my purse. I'll get it. Once you read it, pass it on to the others."

Shrewd blue eyes gave her the once-over. "Are you sure everything is okay?"

No. I'm not. But Liz didn't want to worry her friends anymore than they already were. "Sure. Let me go get the copy."

Liz retraced her steps to the kitchen, still on edge from the delivery of the anonymous note. For now, she'd let her friends dwell on the letter written by Emma while she worried about the letter written asking her to *help* Emma.

The next afternoon, Opal rattled off directions as Liz drove to Althea Mitchell's home. The older woman chatted away, giving a running commentary of passing landmarks, as only someone who had lived in Pleasant Creek all her life could do. When Liz turned the car down Althea's street, Opal angled herself in the passenger seat to face Liz.

"Now remember, Althea is very sought after for her wealth of knowledge, and she's done me a favor by meeting with us. I'm not sure how much time she can spare."

"You told me that back at the inn," Liz said as she parked her black Acura in the circular drive.

By now, all the Material Girls had read the letter. Each had her own take, but everyone agreed it was indeed a love letter and that the romance had been somehow illicit. Naomi picked up on the sense of fear the author conveyed, while Caitlyn, a softy for someone who came off so rebellious, worried about F and how he dealt with the fact he might never see his true love again. Liz had been too preoccupied by the note she'd found in her kitchen to discuss any of the points made by her friends.

"Defer to her," Opal continued. "She's the expert."

"Got it."

"She has a certain personality. It's rather . . . scholarly."

"Is that code for know-it-all?"

Opal's eyes went wide before her lips curved in a sly smile. "Sometimes, yes."

Liz chuckled. From the first time she'd met Opal, the older woman had been on the quiet side. Reserved was probably a better word. Although not Amish, she dressed conservatively and looked at life through that same filter. But after spending more time with Opal, Liz had caught on to the woman's keen but subtle sense of humor.

"I take it you want me to present my photo and letter, and then be quiet and let Althea have at it?"

"Not until after we've asked how things are going with her. She is usually writing a paper or getting ready to travel to a lecture. And she'll be receiving an award at the upcoming Indiana Genealogy Guild banquet. It's very prestigious."

"You said she was renowned."

"And popular. My husband and I sponsored a table at the banquet. I can't wait to hear Althea's speech when she accepts her award."

"That's great, but today?"

"Once she fills us in on her activities, you can bring up today's topic."

"Anything else?"

"I've noticed she doesn't like anyone questioning her interpretations." Opal frowned. "Good thing she's not a teacher. I don't think she'd be very good at it."

I wonder if I'm expected to curtsy. Liz thought wryly. She couldn't wait to meet this woman.

"Suppose she doesn't have answers to my questions? What then?"

Opal blinked. "Oh my. I've never known Althea to be without answers. It would certainly be a first."

"She's that knowledgeable?"

"In her field, yes." Opal's gaze grew troubled. "I hope I haven't painted Althea in too bad a light. She really is a friend."

Liz patted Opal's arm. "I'm sure she is, and I'm sure she'll be wonderful. If she has any information, that's all we can ask for."

In the past day, Liz had reread the letter numerous times and even used a magnifying glass to glean every detail from the photo. With the image enhanced, she was able to confirm the presence of a five-petaled flower on the white background of the broach and identify it as a forget-me-not. With the help of the Internet, Liz had learned that the broach probably had a metal base and porcelain front, the flower depiction most likely hand painted.

But even though Liz was pleased with the results of her research, a whole host of new questions had immediately invaded her thoughts. Did the flower choice have specific meaning? Had the brooch been a gift from the man in the photo? Was the brooch something she could trace?

"Hurry now, we don't want to keep Althea waiting." Opal's smile hinted at her excitement about the upcoming meeting.

The women walked to the front door. Opal rang the bell while Liz took in the surroundings. The colonial-style house was set on what could easily be an acre of land. The pristine white paint and blue trim bestowed a stately air upon the place. The landscaping consisted of trimmed shrubs and flowers in regular, neat rows. The circular driveway had one other car parked in it besides Liz's Acura, an older model brown sedan. No sign of pets or even squirrels.

As Liz finished scrutinizing her surroundings, the door opened. A woman, probably in her early thirties, greeted them with a sunny smile.

"Welcome, Opal. And you must be Liz. Please, come in. Dr. Mitchell is waiting in the living room." She ushered them inside. "I'm Lesley Bishop, Dr. Mitchell's assistant."

"It's good to see you again," Opal said.

"Likewise. Follow me."

As Lesley led the way, Opal leaned toward Liz and whispered, "Assistant number five in two years."

Liz felt her mouth gape. "Are you kidding?"

"Not about Althea's assistants."

Now Liz *really* couldn't wait to meet the woman.

They entered a very formal and well-appointed living room. Stuffy, floral-print furniture filled the room, which was painted a bright blue. Antiques were displayed all around on delicate and well-dusted end tables, tabletops, and bookshelves. On the fireplace mantel Liz noticed two encased collections. One showcased coins, the other held an assortment of jewelry. The jewelry was rather antique-looking in Liz's mind, but being far from an expert, she had no idea. She moved closer, admiring the small works of art.

"Mr. Mitchell's coins," Lesley informed her. "The Mitchells have all kinds of interesting artifacts from their travels." She made a sweeping gesture.

Liz stepped back. Her eyes went wide at the numerous awards framed and mounted on the walls. Liz craned her neck to read the certificates and plaques closest to her. *Genealogy Today* honored Althea for "Outstanding Historical Contributions to Women's Studies." A children's group thanked Althea for time she spent spearheading a community project. Liz imagined the awards hanging on the other walls were pretty much the same—accolades to a woman who shared her time and expertise with others. It looked like Althea had earned the right to be a bit of a know-it-all.

Liz turned around to see Althea Mitchell seated in a high-backed, mauve-color armchair, every bit the queen of her domain. Althea's white hair was teased high above her wrinkled forehead, a red bow fastened to the side. *A piece of whimsy?* Her considerable girth could not be concealed by the flower print dress; her feet were stuffed into white pumps. Althea held a teacup and saucer in her hand, sipping delicately as she observed her callers. A very beautiful teapot and additional cups were placed on the highly polished coffee table near the center of the room.

Althea deposited her cup and saucer on the table beside her chair and rose, tottering slightly. She stretched out both hands in greeting, but stayed glued to her position on the Oriental rug. "Opal, my dear. How lovely of you to call on me."

Opal rushed forward to clasp her friend's hands in hers. "Thank you so much for seeing us, Althea." She nodded toward Liz. "This is my friend Liz, the woman I was telling you about."

Liz walked to Althea, extending her hand. "It's a pleasure to meet you, Dr. Mitchell. I've heard so much about you."

Althea beamed. "I do have a bit of a reputation to uphold."

"As I told Liz," Opal quickly said.

"Please, sit. And do call me Althea."

Liz and Opal took a seat on the couch opposite Althea, who settled back into the regal chair as if to resume court. "Have some tea. Lesley has seen to our visit, but she will get anything that's missing."

"This is fine. We don't want to be a bother."

Althea waved her hand. "No problem at all, Opal. That's why I have Lesley."

Liz shot a glance at Althea's assistant. The woman stood by the door, the same pleasant smile on her face, eager to do her boss's bidding.

According to her script, Opal started asking questions. "Althea, what have you been up to?"

"Research. And plenty of it."

"About?"

"The Ashby side of my family."

"You aren't finished with that project?"

"Heavens no. Too many lectures have been cutting into my writing time. If I were smart, I would decline some of the offers that come in daily, but I don't want to let my admirers down." Althea let out a dramatic sigh. "That being the case, the paper has taken me much longer to finish than I anticipated."

"Will you have it completed before the banquet?"

"Only time will tell." Althea turned her focus to Liz. "Are you interested in history? Genealogy, in particular?"

"A little. I recently went on a journey to find my Amish roots. That's how I ended up in Pleasant Creek."

"It's very rewarding, isn't it?"

"Yes. I found my mother's family and learned a lot about her in the process."

"Family history is very important. I wish more people looked into where they come from and *who* they come from. It shapes much of who we are."

If Althea had her way, she'd never cease to expound on her topic. Liz bit the inside of her cheek and shot a glance at Opal, who nodded.

"Althea," Opal began, "Liz has found something she'd like you to see."

Liz handed the copy of the photo to Althea.

"We were hoping you might recognize the couple in this photo," Liz said. "We think it was taken sometime around the Civil War."

"Let me see." Althea slipped on her reading glasses and studied the picture. After a few moments her brow wrinkled.

"Is something wrong?" Liz asked.

Althea removed her glasses. "How did you come upon this?"

Liz told the story of Beans finding the bones. "Opal suggested you might have some insight into who the people in the photo are."

Althea glanced at the photo again. Liz could have sworn she saw the woman wince. "And this was found with the remains?"

"Yes, but indirectly, we think. The bones were definitely there a long time, but the photo and letter were in a plastic bag, so it's almost certain they were put there recently. I don't even know if they have anything to do with the remains. The whole thing is strange. The police will sort all that out. I just couldn't help but be intrigued by the photo."

Althea nodded as she looked at the picture again.

"Do you recognize the couple?"

Althea squinted at the picture. "This woman looks vaguely familiar."

"Emma."

Althea's head shot up, her gaze cutting to Liz. "You know her name?"

"I assumed that was her name since there is also a letter signed by an Emma."

"Have you heard of her?" Opal queried.

"I come across many names in my work." Althea waved her hand dismissively. "I've been fascinated by Civil War spies lately. Not much is known, I'm afraid, especially not of real names since women weren't technically allowed to enlist in the military then." Althea looked at the print again. "But this woman . . ."

She rose and went to a nearby desk, sifting through a stack of papers.

"This is amazing," Opal said as Althea went through her notes. "Were there many female spies during the war?"

"Probably more than you would think," Althea said over her shoulder. "A few women even dressed like men and fought as part of the military. Most helped the war effort by cooking for the soldiers, sewing or mending uniforms, or giving blankets and raising money for medical supplies."

Opal leaned forward in her chair. "Fascinating."

"Because the men had gone off to fight, many women took over businesses and worked in support of the war effort. Some independent women took it a step further, working in the clandestine world of spies."

"Sounds like an intriguing topic," Opal said. "You should write a paper on the subject. Especially if this woman was from around here."

Althea turned, an apologetic expression on her face. "Sorry. I seem to be mistaken. I don't know her identity after all." She moved to reclaim her seat.

"What about the man?" Liz asked.

Althea shook her head. "I don't recognize him. You said there was a letter?"

Liz passed the photocopy to Althea. She waited patiently for Althea to read it, hoping the woman could shed more light on the mystery. Concern washed over Liz when Althea looked up, her face a mask.

Almost afraid to ask, Liz cleared her throat. "What do you think?"

"I think this letter is meaningless."

What? How could Althea dismiss the longing and fear in every word written? How could she ignore the disappointment of Emma's lot in life? Before Liz could ask any of those questions, Althea spoke again.

"This is clearly a lovesick woman bemoaning her state in life. It contains nothing of real relevance to me or anyone else for that matter."

"I disagree," Liz pushed on, ignoring Opal's warning look. "The author of this letter has poured out her heart to the reader."

Althea's mouth twisted. "Foolish mush. Hardly any historical relevance as far as I can see." She rose, shoving the papers back to Liz as if she couldn't get rid of them fast enough. "I'm going to have to ask you to leave now."

"But I was hoping—"

"I'm afraid I can't help you. This is most likely a dead end." Althea turned to Opal. "I'll see you at the banquet."

If Liz were the suspicious type, she would wonder why the chatty historian had suddenly clammed up.

Opal stumbled over her words. "Um . . . yes . . . the banquet."

"Lesley, please see my guests out."

Lesley hastened to obey, her face flushed as she ushered Liz and Opal to the door.

"I'm so sorry," she said in a quiet tone. "Dr. Mitchell isn't normally so prickly. I don't know what happened to change her mood."

"It's fine," Opal assured her. "Althea has a lot on her plate. We're glad she took the time to see us."

Lesley glanced at Liz. "I hope you aren't too disappointed."

Liz wasn't sure how to best respond, so she simply smiled politely. "I understand Althea is very busy."

"Please call if you need anything else." Lesley opened the front door. "I can help you, or if necessary, I can ask Dr. Mitchell myself."

Liz walked to the car, slipping on her sunglasses to ward off the bright sunlight. What had happened to change Althea's mood? She'd been fine until she read the letter.

"That didn't go well," Opal muttered.

Liz glanced at her friend. "Really?"

"You *did* notice that Althea suddenly became curt and asked us to leave. She's usually so eager to share her expertise, unless someone provokes her."

"Guilty," Liz said, not missing the frown aimed at her. "But your friend still delivered."

Opal's brows rose. "Delivered what?"

"A lead. Call it a hunch, but I think your historian knows far more about this than she's saying."

6

A few hours later, Liz found herself up to her elbows in flour, kneading the lump of dough with more pressure than was necessary to get the job done.

Althea Mitchell was lying to her. Her lawyer's instinct knew it. It was all in the body language. The big question was, why?

And what about the anonymous note? Who wants the truth of Emma's past revealed now?

Liz felt as though she were stuck in a time warp, trying to uncover the secrets of the past while figuring out the very real events in the present.

She punched the dough once more, thinking that the first step in finding out Emma's story hadn't gone as she expected, but at least she felt like she had something to go on now if Althea's first reaction was really the truth. *Female spy?* From the photo, Liz would never have suspected that the severe-looking woman had a secret like that. But maybe she did. Maybe she had more than one secret, in fact. Emma stated in the letter that she couldn't be with the man she loved. And there was a chance that she might have covertly served in the military, possibly as a spy. Every time Liz thought about it, the mystery behind Emma became more and more compelling.

After a few minutes, Liz flipped the lump of dough and began kneading in earnest. Maybe she could find out more in the town records. She could go back through history to see if there was any mention of a woman named Emma around the time of the Civil War. With no last name to go on, the initial inquiry would be broad, but Liz had patience. Althea's mention of female spies had given Liz a starting point.

She'd just pounded the dough again when Mary Ann strolled into the kitchen, a glass in hand.

"What did that dough ever do to you?" Mary Ann asked.

Liz paused, realizing she was taking her frustrations out on the bread. "Kneading is a great stress reliever."

"What are you experimenting with this time?"

"Sourdough bread. Sarah brought me the recipe yesterday."

Liz placed the dough in a pan to rise. She wiped her hands on a towel and then rested her palms on the counter behind her and leaned back. "Did Opal tell you about our visit to see Althea today?"

Mary Ann filled her glass with water from a pitcher in the refrigerator. "Civil War spies? Opal was excited beyond words."

"I never really thought about women spies during the war. It seems like such a . . . modern tactic, but I guess strategy is strategy. Althea said she didn't know who Emma was from the picture. I'm hoping I might find some information about her through county records though."

"Isn't Althea going to help you?"

"No. She was fine when she studied the photo, but when she read the letter she became downright frosty."

"I got the impression Opal was a bit ruffled by your line of questioning to Althea."

"Oh, she was. I think Opal sees Althea as this amazing woman who knows everything about history." Liz paused. "But I got the feeling there was something strange going on with Althea. I can't quite put my finger on it, but it was strange. It was like she couldn't get us out of her house fast enough once she'd read the letter. Even her assistant seemed surprised."

"There's no explaining people's actions sometimes."

"Speaking of people's actions," Liz said as she moved away from the counter, "do you have a few minutes?"

"Sure. Sadie's watching the store."

"Come with me."

Removing her apron and tossing it on the prep table, Liz led Mary Ann to her private living quarters. Once inside, she closed the door behind them and then rounded her desk. She opened the top drawer and removed a piece of paper, handing it to Mary Ann.

Mary Ann arched a brow. "Hmm. I take it this is something serious?"

"I'm not sure. You tell me."

Mary Ann unfolded the paper and read out loud, "Please help Emma." She glanced at Liz. "Where did you get this?"

"I found it on the kitchen island when I got home from the police station."

"And you are just now showing it to me?"

"I meant to, but . . ."

"Did you tell the police?"

"No. It could be nothing."

"And it could be everything. Liz, I don't think this is something to fool around with."

Mary Ann dropped the paper on the desk as if she didn't want to touch it. Liz watched it flutter onto the blotter, the truth behind her friend's words hitting home. Secrecy never did anyone any good. This wasn't the time to start down that road.

"Suppose whoever sent this note came back and confronted you? And what if it turned dangerous? If no one knew about this note," Mary Ann continued, "we would have no idea if something had happened to you. Or why."

"I know. I'm sorry." Liz blew out a long breath. "This is turning into more than I expected."

"Then let the police handle it."

"I'd feel like I was giving up on Emma."

"You don't owe her anything," Mary Ann said. "For heaven's sake, you don't even know her."

"True. But between the bones and the letter, I can't shake the feeling there's so much more to her story. And after Althea's odd reaction, I want to see this through."

"I understand, because I have to admit, I'm intrigued as well. But if you . . . *we* are going to look deeper into Emma's past, you have to promise you won't keep anything from us."

"Agreed."

"The Material Girls will all be at the shop tonight. Miriam is bringing her treadle sewing machine so she can have a trial run-through of her class before we open it up to the public. We can discuss this latest development."

"Sounds like a good idea." Liz placed the note back into her desk drawer as Mary Ann opened the door.

"I'll see you later tonight?"

Liz nodded. "I'll be there."

———————— wwwwwwwwwwwwwwwwww ————————

The Material Girls gathered around the old-fashioned sewing machine, watching as Miriam stitched together pieces of fabric by working the foot pedal. The black machine shone in the overhead lighting, gold filigree lettering with the name "National" scrolled across the arm. Despite its age, the machine was in pristine condition, and Miriam was clearly an expert in its use.

"We already have five women signed up for your Wednesday morning class," Sadie told Miriam. "If interest keeps up, we'll add a Thursday class like we talked about."

"It has been a while since I taught a class, but now that my *Kinders* are getting older, I'm looking forward to it." In contrast to her solemn brown dress, white apron, and black bonnet, Miriam's lively features reflected the excitement in her words. "Tonight is good practice for when I will interact with new students. Taking on a *Steppdecke* project," she paused and looked at Liz, "that is, a quilt project can be time consuming."

The friendly conversation continued as everyone took a turn on the machine before Miriam finished the quilt top and the demonstration ended.

Back to their own projects, the women chatted until Sadie finally put down her needle and fabric. "Liz, you've been quiet all night. What's on your mind?"

Liz looked up to find all eyes on her. "Sorry, everyone. My mind isn't really on sewing tonight."

So much had happened in the past few days. Until she found out more about Emma, and why someone wanted Liz to "help" her, life would be complicated. She glanced up to catch Mary Ann's gaze, interpreting the silent question. *Well? Are you going to tell the others?*

Liz had thought long and hard about it, but she still wasn't sure she was ready to inform the girls about the anonymous note. So she told them about the Civil War spy angle, which they agreed was exciting, and Althea's odd turnabout, which left them stumped as well.

"I'm sorry your visit to Althea didn't give you any specific answers," Sadie said, her attention back to her needlework. "I know Althea tends to be temperamental, but her treatment of you seems downright rude."

"I think we caught her off guard," Opal said in defense of her friend. "Between her papers, going through ancestry files, and getting ready for the awards banquet, she's under a lot of strain. And it wasn't just today. She's been short-tempered at the past few Women in History meetings."

"I didn't take it personally," Liz said. "Reading the letter upset her for some reason. I can certainly cut her some slack."

Miriam continued to sew as she commented, "I could not believe it when I heard that old human bones were found on your property. You must have been shocked, Liz."

"You could say that."

"She handled it like a champ," Sadie said. "Didn't miss a beat dealing with the police or her guests."

"I can attribute that to my law career." Liz chuckled. "I'm trained to handle strange turns of events."

"Still, it must have upset you," Miriam insisted, looking up from her work.

"Yes, but the chief is investigating, so there's not much I can do."

"Except hunt down the identity of this Emma woman," Caitlyn added. "I really hope she was a spy. How cool would that be?"

"Don't get any ideas," Mary Ann warned.

"The closest I would come to anything to do with spies is reading a thriller. The idea is exciting, but I don't think I would blend in like I imagine you'd need to with my red hair." Caitlyn ran a hand through her thick hair. "Probably not a good thing to be too noticeable in the spy trade."

"Just think about it," Naomi said, shaking her head, "these women put their lives on the line for their country, and no one ever even knew about them." She glanced at Liz. "I understand why you want to find out about Emma."

"This is why I'm such an active member of Women in History," said Opal. "The things I find out about brave ladies in our past continually amaze me." She dropped the colorful quilt she was stitching into her lap. "And after hearing how fascinated all of you are by the topic, I have a request."

"Uh-oh," Sadie said. "Here comes the pitch."

"True, Sadie, but for a good cause. You know about the awards banquet coming up. George and I sponsored a table for eight, and I was wondering if any of you would like to attend?"

"When is it?" Caitlyn asked.

"Two weeks from Saturday night."

"I'm in," Sadie piped up right away. It was no surprise really; whenever there was a party, Sadie was the first to arrive and the last to leave.

"Let me check my calendar," Mary Ann told Opal.

"Pretty sure I'm working," Caitlyn said. "I'll see if I can switch my shift."

Naomi nodded. "I'll have to get back to you too."

Miriam declined. "I need to be home to prepare *Stünachta*. My hungry family needs their evening meal."

"Liz?"

For a moment, Liz considered the invitation. Althea would be there, which would give Liz another chance to talk to the woman. Plus, there would be food. She wouldn't turn down a meal she didn't have to cook or clean up after. "Sure. Sounds like fun."

Opal nearly bounced with pleasure in her seat. A smile lit up her face. "So that's a definite "yes" for Sadie and Liz and a "no" for Miriam. If the rest of you will just let me know as soon as possible if you can definitely attend or not, that would be great. It's a table for eight, so we will all fit." Still beaming, Opal folded her quilt and stood. "I should be getting home. George has probably fallen asleep watching one of those train documentaries he likes."

"Me too. The goodies don't bake themselves," Naomi said. "Too bad there aren't any bakery fairies to do the job while I grab a few extra hours of sleep."

"Hey, if I have to be up early to get breakfast ready, so do you," Liz good-naturedly complained. "That way if I burn anything, I can count on you to supply the danish pastries."

Naomi chuckled. "Come to think of it, I've only had to come to your rescue once."

"That was before my eyes got used to focusing in the dark. I'm getting better."

"Mr. Hastings thinks so," Sadie said. "He was in here this morning praising your kitchen skills. How long are they staying, anyway?"

"It was only supposed to be two nights, but they've extended their reservation since the, uh, discovery. Mrs. Hastings wants to know the outcome with Emma."

Mary Ann's brow wrinkled. "That could be a while."

Liz shrugged. "The woman is adamant."

"I say Mr. Hastings only agreed to his wife's idea because he loves your breakfasts," said Sadie.

"As long as rooms are filled, I'm happy. I was really afraid finding the bones would turn potential guests off, but only one person left when they learned about it."

"That's because everyone loves a mystery, Liz," said Mary Ann. "People go on vacation to escape their everyday life. What could be better than a real investigation going on?"

"Yeah," Caitlyn said. "It's not like they have to worry about a murderer lurking around. The bones are old."

"Still, I hope it's not a bad omen." Opal hunted in her purse for her keys.

Liz gathered up her materials to hide the shudder ghosting over her. She didn't believe in omens, but she did know a thing or two about bad press. The reopening of the Olde Mansion Inn didn't need any negative publicity. Not after she'd worked so hard to get the place up and running.

The women said their goodbyes and went their separate ways. After a few minutes, only Mary Ann remained. As she locked the door to Sew Welcome, she asked Liz to hold on a minute.

"You didn't mention the note," she said, joining Liz in the foyer.

"I thought about it, but didn't see any point right now."

"Other than the fact that you don't need to keep this to yourself? You're among friends here."

"Friends I don't want to burden with my problems."

Mary Ann waved her hand. "Nonsense. We're in this together."

"Okay. I'll tell them the next time we meet."

"And the police?"

"I'll contact the chief tomorrow." There was no point in arguing with Mary Ann. The older woman would keep after Liz until she complied.

"Good. Now try to get some sleep."

Liz watched from the porch as Mary Ann walked to the Sew Welcome van and drove away. The evening had grown chilly, a welcome breeze stirring the air. The sweet scent of newly blooming flowers mingled with rich earth. Stars carpeted the sky and insects buzzed as they sought out the porch light in the dark night.

Liz leaned against the doorjamb and sighed. How many nights had she lingered on her high-rise balcony back in Boston? Not many. Her workload and meetings had always served as an excuse to hole up in her law office. Taking time to appreciate the marvels of the world around her had come as a pleasant revelation—one Liz wouldn't take for granted.

With a last look around the quiet grounds, she went back inside, locking the heavy front door behind her.

Since only two rooms were occupied tonight, and she knew her guests had retired earlier, Liz tidied up the sitting room and looked over the dining room one last time to make sure all was in place for the morning before switching off the lights.

Once she reached her quarters, she sank down on the bed and stared at the ceiling, hoping she could finally relax. But it was impossible. Until she knew why someone wanted her to somehow help Emma—whatever that meant—her mind wouldn't stray far from the topic.

Something about the photo nagged at Liz, but she couldn't put her finger on it. And as long as she kept coming up with questions, she would keep searching for answers. Even if she didn't like the results.

7

Liz's alarm clock blared its daily warning, and she forced an eye open. It was still dark and she felt tired from the short night, but she managed to get up and get ready, going through her morning routine as if on autopilot in order to make sure breakfast was ready for her guests when they came downstairs.

Mr. Hastings was thrilled with the sourdough bread, but poor Sarah had to pick up Liz's slack serving since she just couldn't seem to focus. Not that Sarah complained. Liz liked that quality in her young employee.

"My dear, you look like you haven't slept a wink," Mrs. Hastings admonished as Liz nearly dropped a fresh platter of scrambled eggs.

Liz couldn't argue with that. She *felt* like she hadn't slept a wink. Still, she'd dragged herself out of bed because she had a long to-do list. With new guests checking in later that day, the inn would be full for the weekend.

"I imagine all the goings-on around here have you out of sorts," Mrs. Hastings continued. "Even I had a hard time sleeping last night."

"You wouldn't know it with all the snoring going on," her husband teased.

"Donald!" She playfully swatted her husband's arm. "I do *not* snore."

Ignoring his wife's comment, Mr. Hastings said, "I had dreams of that sourdough bread you told me about yesterday, Liz. I couldn't wait to get downstairs this morning to see if you'd added it to the menu. I'm glad you did."

"As if you need more bread," Mrs. Hastings huffed.

Liz laughed. The couple's levity boosted her mood.

"But I don't see you catching up on your shut-eye anytime soon," Mrs. Hastings said, turning her attention to Liz.

"Why is that?"

She pointed out the window. "Looks like someone is trespassing on the crime scene."

Liz glanced outside. Sure enough, a man was walking around to her backyard.

"It's the police chief. Probably following up," she assured her guest. Hurrying into the kitchen, Liz nearly tripped over Beans, who indicated quite clearly that it was time for his breakfast.

"Sorry, buddy, but you started this," Liz said to Beans. "Sarah, would you please feed Beans. Again."

Beans gave a triumphant grunt and sat to wait.

"Is something wrong?" Sarah turned from the sink where she was rinsing off the colorful breakfast plates.

"I'll know in a few minutes." Liz shot out the back door, her long strides taking her to the chief in no time.

He looked up and smiled. "Good morning."

"Is it?" Liz eyed him with a hint of suspicion. "Why are you out here?"

"I like to walk the scene and sort out things." The chief shrugged. "Part of the process."

Liz placed a hand on her hip, not fooled at all. "Chief, what's happened?"

"The plastic bag came back from the lab. Only your prints were found on the outside. The contents had lots of fingerprints. Too many to single out."

"So you're saying you've reached a dead end?"

"Not yet, but this concerns me. Someone deliberately planted the bag. While finding the bones alone is troublesome, they've obviously been in the ground a long time. The bag is the game changer."

"And you're looking for new clues?"

He nodded. "My team went over the area with a fine-tooth comb, but sometimes evidence hides where you least expect it."

The nagging sensation that there was more to the case bothered Liz again. But what could she tell the chief when she hadn't entirely figured it out herself? "I might be able to help you."

The chief's gaze pierced hers, but he said nothing.

"I received an anonymous note."

"When?"

"Two days ago. Someone left it in my kitchen."

"And you didn't feel the need to inform me about it until now?"

Liz looked at the ground. What could she say? Guilty as charged.

"Do you still have the note?" the chief pressed.

She looked up. "It's in my room. Let me go get it."

Liz hurried back inside the inn to fetch the note. When she returned to the backyard, the chief was returning from his car. He held out an evidence bag. Liz dropped the paper inside, and the chief sealed the bag.

"Does anyone else know about this?" he asked.

"Yes. I showed it to Mary Ann."

"Did she touch it?"

"Yes."

He nodded, his expression stern. "Besides the note, are there any other incidents you've neglected to tell me about?"

"No, sir. All I know is that the letter was written right after the Civil War," Liz told him. "I spoke to a local historian, Althea Mitchell, and we're trying to determine if the woman in the picture was a spy."

His brow lifted. "A spy? Makes for titillating conjecture, but honestly, I don't have the manpower to look into the history behind the letter." He held up the bag. "This note is another story altogether."

"While you check it out, I'm planning to dig more into the historical aspect, even though I'm not quite sure where to turn next."

"Look, Liz, I know you want answers. So do we. But this note changes everything."

Her lips formed a mulish line. "I—"

The chief's cell phone pinged. He unhooked it from the holder on his belt and read a text. "Got to get back to the station. Please try to stay out of trouble," he warned as he began walking toward his car.

"I'm not making any promises," she called after him.

When Liz entered the kitchen, Sadie was leaning against the counter, cradling a cup of coffee, a big smile on her face. "Bert Worth."

Liz paused, confused. "Excuse me?"

Sadie placed her cup on the counter. "Since the negative outcome of your meeting at Althea's house, I've racked my brain to think of someone else who would be willing to dig into the matter of Emma. I came up with Bert. He's a retired record keeper. He's also the self-appointed town historian. Bert's got all kinds of memorabilia and historical whatnot."

"Is he someone you trust? I have to say, I was a little disappointed after meeting Althea."

"This is right up his alley, Liz, and you won't need a gilded invitation this time. You couldn't hope for a gentler, happier soul than Bert."

"Sounds promising. Where do I find him?"

"At the courthouse, most days. He has this project idea to display Pleasant Creek history on the main floor, so he's waiting for approval from the town council and making some sketches. Usually he volunteers, talking to tourists and such."

Liz grinned. "Talking is good. Researching is better."

"Then Bert's your man. He's a master at fact-checking and finding obscure information most people overlook." Sadie's gaze met Liz's in what Liz could have sworn was a challenge. "If you're willing . . ."

"Oh, I'm more than willing."

"Great. Go talk to Bert." Sadie refilled her cup. "Let me know if he uncovers anything, no matter how insignificant it might be."

"As if I have a choice in the matter."

Sadie chuckled as she left the kitchen.

Althea might have been unwilling to involve herself, but maybe this Bert Worth would help Liz find answers. At least she had another avenue to search for more information about Emma and the letter.

Hearing chatter from the other room, Liz went back to the dining room and joined her guests. After answering questions about the chief's visit, Mrs. Hastings held up her coffee cup signaling a refill. Duty called. History hunting would have to wait.

Liz and Sarah tackled all the heavy cleaning before the new guests arrived. Then Liz planned the menu for the next few days and brewed iced tea to go with the cookies she'd made to greet the new guests.

With a good two hours to go before her inn was full for the weekend, she took a break to seek out Bert, arriving at the courthouse just after one in the afternoon.

Liz squinted in the bright sunlight and paused to let a black buggy pass by. She nodded in greeting before hurrying to the opposite sidewalk. Just as she jogged up the steps, Jackson came out of the building.

His handsome face broke into a smile when he saw her. "How's the hunt going?"

"Slow. I'm finding out that delving into the past isn't as easy as you might think. Plus, the chief has made it crystal clear that he'd be much happier if I quit searching for answers altogether."

"I don't suppose his suggestion went over well."

"We had to agree to disagree for now. That's why I'm here."

"And I thought you'd stopped by to say hello," he teased.

"Maybe another day. Right now I have business."

Jackson opened the door. "Don't let me hold you up."

Liz met his friendly gaze. "Thanks. Do you know where I can find Bert Worth?"

A knowing smile curved his lips. "I should have guessed. Bert is down the hallway, last room on the right."

"Thank you, Jackson."

"Oh, and one more thing. Did Opal invite you to the awards banquet?"

"She did. I'm planning on going. Why?"

"She asked me as well, so I thought perhaps we could go together. I don't mind attending because Opal asked and it kind of falls under mayoral duties, but to be honest, sitting through another dinner, well, sometimes it's more duty than pleasure. I thought it might be nice to go with someone."

Charmed by his frank admission, Liz said, "I know what you mean. I couldn't let Opal down either." Also, Liz wanted to see how Althea acted among her peers. "Sure. Let's go together. Sounds like fun."

"Okay. I'll get back with you on the particulars." He nodded toward the building. "Good luck."

"If Bert is as good as Sadie says, I won't need it."

"He is."

When Liz reached the room Jackson had directed her to, she found the door wide open. Knocking on the door frame, she called "hello" before walking in.

A short, slim man with glasses and a head covered in fluffy, gray hair looked up from a box. He blinked a few times before stepping back from the desk.

"Can I help you?"

"Yes. My name is Liz Eckardt, I'm—"

"The new owner of the Olde Mansion Inn."

"That's right. My friend Sadie Schwarzentruber steered me your way. I have some historical questions I need answered, and I really hope you can help me."

A big smile lit up his face. "Of course, please come in." Bert glanced around the room. "Don't mind my mess. I've been going through some of my personal collection."

"Sadie said you want to set up a display here."

"I do, but I can't decide what to put on view. It's been a while since I've been through many of these boxes. It's like reuniting with old friends." He shook his cloud of fluffy hair. "But you didn't come to talk about my pet project. What do you want to know, my dear?"

Liz pulled the picture and letter from her purse and explained the circumstances of how they came to be in her possession.

"Ah, yes. I must admit this is not entirely new information to me. You've been the talk of the town. New inn owner finds buried bones on the property. Quite a novel way to make yourself known."

Liz grimaced. "The entire town knows?"

"I suspect so. Speculation is running rampant. But that's the way of small communities."

She handed him the picture first. "I've already spoken to Althea Mitchell. She thought she recognized the woman—Emma—but then she changed her mind. Unfortunately, that was all she could come up with."

Bert studied the photo in silence for a long moment.

Liz bit her bottom lip as she waited for him to speak, not wanting to disturb his train of thought but feeling impatient for an answer. Would this be another dead end?

Finally, Bert tapped his temple. "Emma, Emma . . .? Oh, yes." Carefully placing the copy on the desk, he hurried over to the corner of the room, moved two stacked boxes to get to the third one on the bottom. He gently opened the flap, pulling an old book from inside. Flipping through the pages, he found what he was looking for and handed the book to Liz. She grabbed it with both hands, watching as Bert pointed to a long list of names.

"A few years ago our local church transferred some of the old birth and marriage records to digital. I've always been fascinated by the Civil War era, so I asked to keep the old books. The handwritten entries are so much more personal." He moved his finger to the bottom of the page. "Emma Ashby. Wife of John Ashby."

"You think she's from around here?"

"Most definitely. I assume that's why Althea would have recognized her name. She was the only Emma in Pleasant Creek during the Civil War years, strange as it sounds. Our population was pretty low then. I wonder why Althea didn't tell you as much."

"She said she thought that Emma might have been a spy during the war."

"Interesting. I've looked into female Civil War spies, but it's difficult to confirm unless you have access to family documents. Personal letters usually provide links to the truth behind the rumors. If you were going to tell anyone the truth, wouldn't it be your family?"

"You would think." Liz had stumbled on the truth of her mother's heritage when she found Abigail's journal after she died. That truth, written in those old pages, had wielded enough power to get Liz to move from Boston to Indiana, all because she wanted to seek out her mother's Amish family—*her* Amish family.

"Family records play an important part in verifying history," Bert said. "Where would genealogy experts be without them? Everything from birth and death records, marriage certificates, military service—it all aids the process. It's quite a fascinating study. Once you get hooked, it's hard not to keep digging to find out more about your ancestors."

"So you're saying there must be records of Emma Ashby somewhere. And the fact that she was a local woman plays right into our hands?"

"It certainly makes fact-finding easier. In theory, anyway."

"Would you be willing to help me? Point me in the right direction to start my quest into Emma's past?"

Bert grinned. "It would be a privilege. I love uncovering new information about our former town residents."

"That would be why you're the self-appointed town historian?"

"Is that what they call me?" Bert's bushy eyebrows angled together in a delighted question.

"Sadie," Liz said, the one word carrying all the explanation needed.

Bert chuckled. "Of course. But I can assure you, it's more than a hobby. I keep detailed notes. Between the town settlers and the Amish community, there's a great deal of information to catalog." He nodded to the copy of the letter still in her hand. "May I?"

"Yes! I almost forgot." Liz handed him the letter, waiting for his reaction as he read its contents.

Once he'd read it through, Bert's expression was grim. "This certainly puts a new spin on the situation."

"Now you know why I'm so anxious to find out more." Liz took the letter he handed back to her.

Bert picked up the picture, once again studying the couple. "Odd. Through her detailed family studies, Althea surely knows more about Emma than she's letting on." His serious eyes caught hers. "You do know Althea is an Ashby descendant."

"That's right!" Liz's eyes lit up. "She *did* mention the name Ashby." *Althea* had *known who Emma was.* "If Althea knew this, why did she pretend otherwise when I showed her the picture?"

Bert adjusted the glasses on his nose. "If I had my guess, I'd say it's because the man standing beside Emma in this picture is not her husband."

8

Liz took the photocopy from Bert and held it up in the air. "This man is not John Ashby?"

"No."

"Are you sure?"

Bert chuckled. "I've seen many pictures of the Ashby family. Althea has more than a few on display at her home. The original Ashby home, I might add."

Stunned, Liz looked at the photocopy and then back to Bert. "Do you know who this man is?"

"I'm afraid not. I've never seen him before."

Althea's reaction made more sense now. She knew the man in the photo wasn't her ancestor, which meant she knew the speculation that would come from a picture of Emma with a man who wasn't her husband. It was possible that Althea wouldn't want anyone to know this detail about her family tree, particularly given how proud she was of her spotless pedigree.

Liz shook her head, remembering the visit. "Althea couldn't wait to get us out of her house after she read the letter."

"I can see why."

"Surely she knows I'll put two and two together?"

"She may not. Althea has a high opinion of her . . . family status. And given her multiple degrees in history, she may assume that once she gave you an answer, it was definitive. She probably thinks her final word closes the subject."

"I understand she's a respected historian, but to deliberately misguide me? Isn't that against some professional code of ethics?"

"Historians have been rewriting history ever since someone decided to paint on a cave wall."

"I'm dumbfounded that she lied to me. And to her friend Opal."

"Liz, one of the tricky things about discovering your family roots are the revelations that come with it. Not having actually been there still leaves much out of the equation. Families may think they know everything about their ancestors, and then one piece of information like that letter blows it all away. Especially with no one to answer questions. For someone as accomplished as Althea, this is a big deal, and not in a good way."

Liz knew how it felt to have her entire life changed by having new information about her heritage revealed. The surprising truth in her mother's journal had done just that, so she could understand Althea's shock at learning something previously unknown about her family. Particularly as the new information seemed to cast at least one of her ancestors in a scandalous light. Althea obviously held her family tree in high regard, which supported the lofty esteem she held for herself. What Liz couldn't get over was being lied to, right to her face.

"Are you going to continue to look into Emma's past?" Bert asked.

"Definitely. But I think I need to pay Althea another visit first."

———————————

Liz rang Althea's doorbell again, this time with far more zeal. She'd driven straight to Althea's house from Bert's office. She wanted answers, and she wanted them now.

She was about to press the bell a third time when the door opened. Lesley, Althea's assistant, appeared, a wary expression on her face.

"Ms. Eckardt. I don't recall you setting up another appointment with Dr. Mitchell."

"I didn't." Without being invited, Liz crossed the threshold. "But it's very important that I speak to Althea. Immediately."

Lesley still stood by the open door. "Th-this is highly unorthodox. Dr. Mitchell is busy and—"

A voice carried from down the hallway. "It's okay, Lesley. Please show our visitor in."

Her expression shifting from apprehension to blatant displeasure, Lesley motioned for Liz to follow her. Althea was waiting for them in the living room. She stood by the window, her face drawn as Liz entered. Althea nodded to Lesley who quietly stepped out of the room.

"When I heard you'd gone to visit Bert," Althea said, "I knew it was only a matter of time before you came back."

Goodness. Does everyone in town know my business? "Why weren't you honest with me in the first place?"

"Let me explain." Althea moved to her chair. "Please, take a seat."

Liz did, placing her purse beside her on the couch. "You know who Emma is."

"Yes. When you showed me the photocopy, I knew immediately. The gentleman, however, caught me off guard."

At Althea's shaken tone, Liz forced herself to calm down. Bert was right. This news had thrown the woman for a loop.

"Because he wasn't Emma's husband," Liz said.

Althea nodded. She slumped in the chair slightly and closed her eyes for a moment. Then she straightened up and opened her eyes. "When you gave me the letter, I realized there was more to her than my family ever knew. Secrets are not pleasant to me, Liz."

"You never suspected anything from your research about Emma?"

"No. She was only married to my great-great-great-grandfather for a few short years after the war. "

"Were you ever really checking to see if Emma was a spy?" Liz asked.

"Oh yes. That has been a story carried down through the family line for decades. I didn't make that up."

"Did you find any proof?"

"No." Althea waved a hand. "You have to understand genealogy. It is long, tedious work. Many times it branches out into rabbit trails that don't lead anywhere."

"But don't you have all your family's papers to go by?"

"To a certain extent, yes. John Ashby kept scrupulous records, both personally and for his many businesses. The only problem is, in all of the family documents, I've only come across John and Emma's marriage certificate, a wedding picture, and her death certificate. She was buried in the family plot. But there are no letters. None of her belongings. Nothing allowing me to determine who she was as a person."

"Was she young when she died?"

"In her twenties." Althea sniffed. "She contracted some sort of unpleasant illness."

As if any illness is pleasant. "And that's it? Nothing more?"

"It is strange, but yes. Like I said, my ancestors, John in particular, kept good records."

"Are there birth records of her children with John?"

"They didn't have any children." Althea let out a deep breath. "My line comes from John and his second wife, Annalise."

Liz thought of the photocopy in her purse. "Did Emma have children with anyone else?"

Althea straightened, her features slowly morphing into a thundercloud. "No."

"You can't be shocked by my question. She was photographed with another man and wrote him a love letter. It's a natural assumption."

"Get that idea out of your head immediately," Althea snapped. "We don't know the true reason behind the picture or the letter."

They did, but Liz realized this line of questioning would get her nowhere. "Do you know anything about what went on while Emma and John were married? Were they happy?"

"By all accounts they had an uneventful marriage."

Vague. In other words, the family didn't know or they weren't saying. "Althea, I know this is upsetting to you. But if we can figure this out—"

"I will not have my family name sullied by false conclusions drawn from scant evidence."

Liz had the distinct feeling that she had just been outranked and put in her place.

Althea stood slowly as if all her energy had been sapped. "Please, I'd rather not continue this conversation. Lesley will see you out." She left the room without a backward glance.

Shaking her head, Liz rose and rounded the couch. Her gaze landed on the other certificates and awards she'd missed the first time she'd visited. Curious, Liz did a quick walk around the room, reading one after another, until she reached the mantel. She gave the coin collection a cursory scan, but something else was tugging at her gaze—the jewelry collection. Before Lesley arrived, Liz took a few moments to study the dozen or so pieces displayed in a glass-fronted box, from silver filigree earrings to heavy-stoned rings, watches, and charm bracelets. Mixed into the collection were a few pins. About half were metal, a few almost crude in construction, as if they were very old. Some were fronted with porcelain on which there were hand-painted themes from flowers to birds.

Liz examined each piece of jewelry, but one brooch in particular caught her eye. The one with a faded forget-me-not flower. She'd seen that pattern before.

Digging into her purse, she withdrew the picture she'd pored over so many times. There could be no mistake. The brooch in the display case was exactly like the one pinned to the neckline of Emma's dress.

"Ms. Eckardt, I'll see you out now."

Liz jumped. She stuffed the paper into her purse as she turned, trying to keep a pleasant expression on her face. "Lovely collection," she said in as even a tone as she could muster.

Lesley looked over Liz's shoulder and smiled. "The current Mitchells have many diverse interests, but I believe that particular grouping belonged to one of the more distant relatives."

That made sense. Emma had been a part of the family at one time.

It was only natural her husband would have kept her jewelry. So much for jumping to conclusions.

Liz joined the assistant, and they walked to the front door. "You must find working for Althea fascinating."

Lesley smiled, but Liz noticed it didn't quite reach her eyes. "She keeps me busy."

Dazzling sunlight greeted them when Lesley opened the front door. As Liz walked out, the younger woman stepped onto the porch behind her and closed the door. Smile in place, this time her expression could only be described as pleasant. Had it been Liz's imagination to think Lesley might be unhappy working for Althea? Or was it the bad lighting in the hallway?

"Can I have a minute of your time?" she asked Liz.

"Of course."

"How do I begin?" Lesley tossed her long brown hair over her shoulder. "Since you visited last, Althea's been on edge. I know she's nervous about the banquet, but she's been more unsettled than usual. I suspect her mood has something to do with your previous visit." Lesley glanced to the house and back again. "Dr. Mitchell is very protective of her family history."

"I can tell."

"Then, may I ask a favor of you?"

"It depends."

Lesley laughed. "Nothing dire. I only ask that you don't interrupt Dr. Mitchell again, at least not until after the banquet. She's looking so forward to it. I'd hate for her big night to be ruined by whatever is going on."

Liz studied the girl for a moment before nodding. "I'll try my best."

Lesley beamed at Liz's answer. "Are you going to keep looking into Dr. Mitchell's family, even if it means doing so without her?"

"I am."

"I have to confess, I overheard some of your conversation. I can tell you that Dr. Mitchell won't be much more help. I can give you the name of another historian I know. She lives nearby and would be happy to help with research. We went to college together, so I can vouch for her." Lesley handed Liz a slip of paper with a name and phone number.

After glancing at it, Liz looked back at her in confusion. "Why . . .?"

"I'm doing this for Dr. Mitchell. If she won't help you, I want you to deal with someone who knows Dr. Mitchell's reputation and will be fair and helpful."

Liz thought of Bert. "I have someone I trust."

"Okay, well, my friend is also involved in women's studies like Dr. Mitchell. So, if you need someone who knows the ropes . . ."

Liz looked at the paper. "Thank you. I'll keep this in mind."

"Please know I'm not doing anything behind Dr. Mitchell's back. She needs a break. All of this pressure is causing her a lot of distress."

Liz suddenly felt guilty. She wanted answers, but not at the expense of another person's health. "I'm sorry. I didn't intend for her to be upset."

"Well, now that you know, we can take steps to minimize Dr. Mitchell's stress. Agreed?"

"Agreed."

Lesley nodded and reached for the doorknob. "Thank you, Liz." Then she turned and entered the house, leaving Liz alone and a little confused on the porch.

Was Liz wrong to pursue this so tenaciously, seeking answers that caused another woman stress and might disparage her family legacy? Liz remembered Althea's distraught expression and couldn't help but wonder if she'd gone too far.

Helping Emma, as the anonymous note's author asked, certainly wasn't in Althea's best interest. And if someone wanted the truth known, why not step forward themselves instead of urging Liz to do the job? The police chief was right. He and his men should look into it.

But did Liz have it in her to stop searching for the truth about Emma?

9

Late Saturday morning, Liz finished cleaning the Sunrise Room, decorated in a blend of contemporary and antique furnishings that warmed in the early morning light. She found exercise to be a great way to think through her problems. Back in Boston, Liz would run whenever she had the chance. Here, housekeeping was her physical exertion of choice. Not only did the chores increase her heart rate, but she also experienced a sense of well-being from taking care of the inn and, by extension, her guests.

Unable to resist pursuing the mystery of Emma, Liz had called Lesley's friend the night before. Julie Sonders sounded both honored and excited that Liz would seek her out. They'd arranged to meet at The Coffee Cup later that afternoon. But first, she had work to do.

Toting a laundry basket full of towels, Liz traipsed down the stairs, stopping in the foyer to greet Mrs. Hastings.

"Liz, my dear. That was another scrumptious breakfast."

"Thank you."

"I do have some news though. Mr. Hastings insists we return home, so we will be checking out today."

"I'm sorry to hear that. Although, it was lovely you stayed longer than planned."

"We do so like it here. And I would never leave you in your time of need, but I certainly don't want to argue with Donald."

Liz smiled. Somehow the Hastingses had come to look at her as a daughter of sorts. How touching.

"Then I can't wait for your return visit."

"Which may be sooner than you think."

"Oh?"

"I'll be back in time for the Indiana Genealogy Guild banquet. If you would please check your reservation schedule? I'd like to book a room for that weekend."

"Are you going to the banquet?"

"No, but I'm hoping you'll get more details that night. I want to be in on it."

Liz chuckled. "I could just call you."

"Where's the fun in that? No, I want to be here in person."

"Okay." Liz walked to the reception desk and pulled out her reservation book. She flipped through the pages to the desired date, two weeks away, and found a room available. "You're all set."

"Wonderful! Now, I must get back to Donald. He's not the neatest packer in the world."

Liz smiled. "That's why he has you to take care of him."

"Truer words were never spoken."

As Mrs. Hastings returned upstairs, Liz continued with her chores. Sarah had the weekend off, so Liz would spend more time on the household duties than usual. She got the wash going and returned to the kitchen to pour herself a cup of coffee. Checking her to-do list, she saw vacuuming came next. Hardly glamorous, but her sense of pride had her working up a sweat she actually enjoyed.

By one o'clock, Liz had taken a shower and dressed in a pink top, white capris, and pink sandals, and was making her way to the coffee shop to meet Julie Sonders.

The weekend crowd filled Main Street. Now that the outdoor temperatures had grown more pleasant and the rains had ceased, the boutique shops were bustling with business. Sweet Everything, Naomi's bakery, had a steady stream of customers. Liz sighed in contentment. She'd really taken to living in Pleasant Creek. The residents had embraced Liz as one of their own, the Material Girls had befriended her right away, and Liz's Amish family was slowly including her in their ranks. She couldn't ask for anything more.

Well, she could. Answers about Emma. Hopefully her new contact would be able to help with that.

Before reaching the coffee shop, she spotted Jackson. He was helping a group of Amish men remove a beautifully crafted cabinet from a wagon. Jackson ran his hand over the grain of the wood as he spoke to what appeared to be the oldest man. When he looked up and noticed Liz, he broke into a smile.

After excusing himself, he strode her way. "A day on the town?"

"Business."

His brow arched in reply.

"I have a new lead about my mysterious couple."

"It sounds like Bert came through for you."

Liz nodded. "I've also found an academic to help out."

"I thought Althea was your academic expert."

"She's been a bit . . . reluctant to continue with this line of research, so I found another historian who specializes in women's studies."

"You are tenacious," Jackson said, a gleam in his eye.

"You say that like it's a bad thing."

Jackson chuckled. "Just stating a fact."

"Then wish me luck. I'm meeting her now."

"I hope you find what you're looking for."

Liz took a few steps away and then stopped and turned to face Jackson again. "You know, I'd like to buy something from your store to have at the inn. Maybe another rocking chair like the one you fixed for me? A matching style perhaps?"

"Come by and view the inventory. Or I'd be happy to have a piece specially made."

"I'll stop by. Thanks." Liz waved goodbye and hurried to her appointment.

As she entered the coffee shop, her gaze roamed the room. Julie had told Liz her blond hair would be pulled back in a ponytail. Soon Liz spotted a woman in her late-twenties that she guessed to be Julie. As she approached, the ponytailed woman stood, all smiles.

"You must be Liz."

"Julie? So pleased to meet you."

"I saved us a table but didn't order yet."

"Let me take care of that, and then we can get down to business."

Liz ordered iced coffees for them both and then rejoined Julie.

"So," Liz said as she took a seat, "tell me about yourself."

Julie scooted to the end of her seat. "I graduated with honors from DePauw University. I didn't initially pursue a graduate degree because I wanted to get out in the field, but I've recently decided to get my doctorate."

"What else have you been doing?"

"I edit papers for publication, although I'm branching out by taking speaking engagements. I recently narrated a friend's film, which he hopes to have picked up by a major network."

"How interesting." Liz took a drink of her coffee. "Are you on board with finding out more about my mysterious Emma?"

"Oh yes. An opportunity like this is a dream come true for a historian. If it turns out well, I might get published in one of the academic journals, which would go a long way toward establishing my name in the field."

"Great. It sounds like you're as motivated as I am to get to the bottom of Emma's story."

Julie nodded. "Of course that's the primary objective."

Liz was a little surprised by Julie's unabashed scholarly ambitions. She was reminded of her law-school days when everyone had fantasies of going to a top firm and making partner. In the end, most of her classmates settled into comfortable private practices. Some went in different directions altogether; although, she hadn't heard of *anyone* else who was running an inn in Amish country.

Liz took the folder from her purse and slid it across the table. "I made a copy of the photo and letter for you. The quality isn't great since they're copies of copies, but it should work."

"It's a good starting point. I've already begun work, reaching out to contacts to get the ball rolling."

"Impressive. I just called you last night."

"You piqued my curiosity." Julie opened the folder to scan the contents. "Looking into the past can be time-consuming. You can't just type a name into the computer and come up with tons of information. A search engine can only find information that's already been fed into it. As a historian, I've developed a network of friends who work at other universities, libraries, and public-record offices."

"You have all the bases covered."

"And you have the best start. A photo and letter. Personal items are always wonderful sources," Julie said. "If a family keeps well-documented records, it's like finding gold. Do you know where the photo and letter originate?"

"That's the question of the hour. I'm afraid I have no idea."

"No worries. Like I said, this is a good start." As Julie took a moment to read the letter, Liz sipped her chilled coffee. "Well, this is certainly compelling." She glanced at Liz. "Especially after you told me on the phone of your suspicion that Emma was married to one of Dr. Mitchell's ancestors."

"Yes, Althea was able to confirm that much."

A smile flashed over Julie's lips so quickly that Liz wondered if she'd imagined it.

"With any luck," Julie said, "I'll be able to find answers for you."

"Good. At least now I'm not the only one excited about digging up the truth."

Julie's nose wrinkled at the poor choice of words. "Is it true you found human remains on your property?"

"Unfortunately, yes. The police are looking into them and the letter, but I'm not sure they have the manpower to focus on a detailed historical investigation."

"Do you think the letter is related to the bones?"

"We don't have all the facts just yet, but I would assume so."

"In honor of whoever might have been buried there," Julie said, "I'm happy to be a part of your project."

"Good. So what happens next?"

"I get back to my sources and keep looking for information. While I was waiting for you I got a text from a friend who may have a lead on Emma's activities during the war. I won't be able to reach him until Monday, but as soon as I learn something, I'll let you know."

"Okay." Liz rose and gathered her purse. "I'll look forward to hearing from you."

"If you don't mind my asking, are there others working on this project?"

"I do have another source of information, yes."

"I know Lesley wouldn't have given you my name if Dr. Mitchell could help you. Don't get me wrong, it's an honor just to have Dr. Mitchell acknowledge the project. Her stamp of approval will open doors for me. For us," she quickly added.

Liz chose not to expand on the situation or what Althea's reaction had been. "I'm just glad it all worked out."

"It is curious though. Dr. Mitchell not being involved, I mean." Julie's eyes narrowed for a fraction of a moment before she returned to her sunny self. "Her reputation is legendary. Big shoes to fill, but I'm up for the job."

As they parted ways, Liz tried to brush off the uneasy feeling niggling at her.

———— ///////////////////////// ————

Liz returned to the inn, ready to greet two young couples checking in as first-time visitors. After making sure they sampled her snacks and showing them to their rooms, she spent the remainder of the afternoon catching up on paperwork. Once evening rolled around, she stopped into Sew Welcome to catch up with her friends.

"Where have you been?" Sadie asked, her purse in one hand, keys in the other.

"You forgot, didn't you?" Mary Ann shook her head and turned to Sadie. "She forgot."

"Okay, I'll admit I forgot." Liz's gaze went back and forth between the two exasperated expressions. "What did I forget?"

"It's cupcake night. We promised Naomi we'd serve."

Liz gave herself a mental head slap. Of course. On the second Saturday of the month, running from April through October, Naomi and the other Main Street restaurants and food specialty stores gave away sample goodies for two hours. In Naomi's case it was mini cupcakes from her bakery. The line for the treats usually spread down the sidewalk. Anyone with a sweet tooth patiently waited for one of the mini cupcakes until Naomi ran out.

Foodie Night, as it had been dubbed, was a hit with the tourists and the locals. Since the weather had turned warm, whole families came out to sample the treats and enjoy a night on the town.

"Let me run to my room and change my shoes. It'll only take a minute."

Sadie sighed dramatically. "We don't want to miss all the fun."

Liz hurried to her room, kicked off her sandals, and slipped into ballet flats. She returned to her friends in record time and apologized profusely as Sadie led the march down the inn walkway.

Mary Ann waved her hand. "You've been busy."

"Yes, but that's no excuse to let Naomi down. Ever since Beans's discovery, she's called every day just to lift my spirits. And here I go forgetting the only time she ever asks for something."

"Don't beat yourself up," Sadie commanded. "You're here now."

Within minutes they reached Naomi's booth. She'd already set up the banner behind the table, the name of the bakery proclaimed in bold coral and green lettering. Sweet Everything's menu listed her inventory so that anyone not familiar with the bakery would see what she had to offer. Her dark hair pulled back, Naomi placed the mini cupcakes in a stand while Caitlyn set a serving dish on the table, ready to start handing out the goodies.

"Where have you been?" Caitlyn teased as the women approached. Liz grimaced and prepared to confess, but Sadie spoke first.

"Just running late," the older woman answered as she took her place behind the booth.

Naomi handed Liz and Mary Ann each a silver platter with cupcakes to pass out. Opal was busy organizing the trays, but when Liz caught her gaze she was troubled by the chill in her friend's eyes. *It looks like I've managed to upset both Althea and Opal.*

"The tourists are really out in force," Naomi said, her face lit with excitement. "This is good since I've been baking up a storm all day."

Liz glanced into the shop and saw that Naomi wasn't kidding. The display cases were filled to capacity.

A trickle of people turned into a stream and then a line. Time flew by as Liz handed out cupcakes and spoke with visitors, welcoming them to Pleasant Creek and directing them into Sweet Everything whenever possible. A group of retirees from the senior center chatted her up about the inn, and some of the women she knew to be regulars at Sew Welcome dropped by the booth. Liz barely had time to catch her breath before Naomi ran out of her treats, only a few minutes before the two hours were up.

"Another successful Foodie Night," Caitlyn said as they packed up.

"And I ran out of cupcakes." Naomi chuckled. "Not that I'm bragging or anything."

"You should brag." Caitlyn brushed a lock of red hair out of her eyes. "I swiped one before we started. I think this was your best batch ever."

"Well, I hope we recruited a few new regular customers tonight."

"I heard several people talking about placing orders," Liz told her friend.

"Hey," Naomi said to Liz, "I saw you walk past the bakery earlier, but I was with a customer so I couldn't leave to catch up to you to talk. Where were you off to?"

Liz wiped a platter with a damp cloth. "I met a historian at the coffee shop."

"Althea?" Opal asked, clearly surprised.

"Bert," Sadie replied.

"Neither," Liz corrected. "Someone different."

Naomi studied her. "You're determined."

"Yes, but . . ." Liz looked at her friends. "Do you think I'm getting too emotionally involved in this?"

"I guess it depends," Mary Ann said.

"What do you mean?"

"You've already upset Althea. Are you willing to do the same to anyone else? Is finding out the truth that important to you?"

Liz caught Opal's gaze. The same questions were mirrored in the older woman's eyes before she turned away to help Naomi fold up the table.

Am I willing to upset anyone else? Liz considered that for a few moments. She hadn't known her new friends for very long, but these women were important to her. Was she willing to risk alienating them over an old love letter from some long-dead woman whose bones might have been buried on her property?

10

The next day, Liz didn't have time to think about the past mysteries affecting her current life as it was filled with tourists streaming in and out of the inn and Sew Welcome.

Sadie had scheduled a late-morning class at the request of returning customers. Liz only caught sight of a few of the women attending the quilting class in between pouring coffee and making sure to replenish her newest breakfast creation, a scrumptious sausage, cheese, and potato casserole. Mary Ann told her the class was mainly ladies who worked during the week but who had set aside some personal creative time on Sunday, joining with retirees wanting to get out and mingle. The class aimed to assist women with their quilting, but it clearly served as a social outlet. Sadie was hoping it would become a regular event. If she wasn't so busy, Liz would have loved to stop in and add a few more hours of stitching on her bedspread.

By Monday, the guests had checked out leaving Liz and Sarah with major cleanup. Liz was in the Somewhere in Time Room, gathering up the linens and towels. She lingered for a moment to study the different clocks scattered about the room, which seemed to give it a more masculine feel. Her gaze settled on one of the clocks, and its ticking reminded her that she hadn't gotten any further with Emma's mystery. Catapulted back to reality, Liz hastened her step, eager to finish the housework so she could continue her research.

On Tuesday morning, as she took a much-needed coffee break, Liz heard from Julie. The young historian called, eager to share her findings. Liz invited her to the inn for lunch so they could catch up.

Checking her watch, Liz realized she had a few chores left before Julie arrived. *Time to get to it.* Rooms didn't clean themselves, and dogs certainly didn't take bologna, Beans's favorite treat, out of the refrigerator on their own.

———————— //////////////////////// ————————

Liz offered Julie a seat in the dining room where she had set out sandwiches and macaroni salad for lunch. Without any guests currently residing, they ate in peace while chatting amiably before moving to the four-season room to get to the topic of Emma.

"I didn't think you'd find something this quickly," Liz said to Julie as they settled in.

"A good friend works for the Indiana State Archives. They have a huge collection of records dating back to the Civil War that they organize and preserve, so my friend has spent years reading about the Union and Confederate armies. She found a lot of information on Indiana volunteer regiments, including roll records, a list of soldiers, and details on the war efforts."

"What did she find on Emma?"

Julie withdrew a few loose papers from her briefcase. "At first, we couldn't make a connection. I was looking for Emma Ashby when it occurred to me she hadn't married until after the war. I called the local records office, and they were able to find her wedding certificate, giving me her maiden name—Emma Hartsfeld. I then went back to the list of soldiers and found this." She pointed to one page in particular. "E. Hartsfeld joined the army in 1862. Since women couldn't enlist, I suspect she disguised herself as a teenage boy and used her first initial to cover the fact that she wasn't a man."

Liz read the list, silently acknowledging all the men and women who had given service in America's history.

"From there I compared names among the lists of regiments with 'special services.' Obviously, 'special' in this case meant secretive, but we were still able to locate records. E. Hartsfeld was labeled 'clandestine' and listed as gaining classified information from the Confederate military."

"So we have proof."

Julie nodded. "It gets better. I found a photo in the military archives dating back to about the time Emma enlisted." She handed another paper to Liz of a degraded photo of uniformed men. "The picture resolution is terrible, but look at the names listed below. E. Hartsfeld is third from the left."

Liz went to retrieve the magnifying glass from her room. When she returned, she studied the soldiers. In uniform, with caps shadowing their faces, Liz couldn't be sure if this E. Hartsfeld was the same woman in the photo Liz had found buried under her lilacs. "I guess we'll have to go with the written record because I can't tell if this is Emma."

"One of the many problems of working with old documents."

"Were you able to find anything else?" Liz asked.

"Unfortunately, not much. I have a copy of Hartsfeld's discharge papers. There was nothing about Emma's job during the war—if that really is her—nor where Hartsfeld might have been stationed or moved with the regiment."

"How about John Ashby?"

"Now he's an open book." Julie removed a stack of papers from her bag. "I easily found birth, death, family, and military records on John. He served in the Union army with distinction. There's nothing untoward about the man."

"A pillar of society?'

"So it would seem."

"Do I detect disbelief in your tone?"

Julie scooted forward on the seat cushion. "The fact that Althea Mitchell is a direct descendant of John Ashby, and she doesn't want to talk about him or Emma has given me some concerns."

"Normally you'd take it all at face value?"

"I would," Julie said as she leaned back and made her case. "Althea has always been proud of her roots. She's writing a paper on the Ashbys for publication. Emma is part of their story. What does Althea have to hide?"

Liz thought for a moment. "Initially, she didn't tell me that Emma was married to John."

"*Exactly.*" Julie's face grew more animated. "When you uncover bits and pieces of history, you want to tell everyone about it. As far as I know, Althea has never hidden her findings before. If she had, she wouldn't be so successful."

"Perhaps it's different when dealing with one's own roots."

Julie riffled through the scattered papers on the coffee table until she found the photo of the person they assumed was Emma standing in the group of soldiers. She held it up for Liz to see. "Perhaps. But I'm not the only one who asked for this information. My friend at the archives had a similar request months ago."

Liz's stomach dipped. "Let me guess. Althea Mitchell?"

"Bingo. She knew all about Emma's secret military history even before you sought her out."

Liz rose from her chair and crossed the room to look out the window toward the bench in the backyard. After the police chief had given her the okay, she'd cleaned up the mess, and with her employee Kiera's help, she'd even gotten her lilac bushes back in shape. She'd also undertaken a mystery while being blocked or discouraged at nearly every turn. Why did it bother her so much that Althea hadn't been forthright? It wasn't like she knew the woman before Opal mentioned her name. Yet, still, she'd hoped for more from a professional historian.

Julie walked up beside Liz and spoke in a measured tone. "Let's assume there's more going on with Althea than she's letting on."

"Let's," Liz said, giving Julie permission to speculate.

"Althea has always prided herself on her family's good reputation. If the man in the photo with Emma was a love interest, it would certainly taint Althea's past."

"All the more reason to cover it up. But still, it was so long ago . . ."

"If she can get you to drop your inquiry, she protects the family name and preserves the integrity of her years of Ashby research."

Liz frowned. "And does something even worse."

"Which is?"

"Covers up a true piece of history."

Julie hesitated before saying, "You think she knows more about the remains found on your property. Do you have reason to think they're Emma's?"

"Althea told me Emma was buried in the family plot. Even if Althea had an idea of whose bones Beans found, I doubt she would reveal the truth now. She's made it clear she doesn't want any more interference."

"Which means we probe deeper."

Exactly what Liz wanted to do, but she didn't want to hurt Althea or alienate Opal in the process.

"Liz, I hope you don't mind if I write about this experience."

"Why don't we wait until the police have answers?"

"I would never push you, but in my world the first one to publish a paper on new information gets the credit."

"There are other considerations besides credit though," Liz said. Certainly, Julie could do what she wanted with her research findings, but Liz would prefer that she tread lightly until they knew more.

Julie quickly backed down. "Of course. Please, let me know when the time is right."

Both promised to be in touch if any new information surfaced, and Liz saw Julie out. Liz wondered how far the eager historian would go to build her professional reputation. Why on earth had Dr. Mitchell's assistant Lesley suggested her? Probably because Julie had access to information, as she'd proved by this visit. The woman was competent.

As Liz closed the door, two women walked out of Sew Welcome. She nodded hello. Then two more women walked past, waving her way. Liz remembered Mary Ann mentioning an advanced quilting class today. She turned on her heel and strode into the shop.

"How did it go?" she asked, heading to the counter.

"Great," Mary Ann said. "All of the women were ready to get busy."

"And not a bit shy with their wallets," Sadie chimed in.

"Sadie, really," Mary Ann admonished while Liz laughed.

"I call 'em like I see 'em."

"Please," Liz said. "Don't ever change."

"I'm a bit too old for that."

"Was that the historian?" Mary Ann asked as she placed her quilting tools in a woven basket.

Liz nodded. "Julie. She's already found information about Emma." Liz quickly summarized what she'd learned.

"Seems to me you should also be looking into the bones," Sadie said.

"Believe me, I agree. But the chief is investigating the bones, and let's face it, the police have the facilities and the people trained to learn what there is to know from the bones and I don't, so I'm stuck on that front. Right now I have leads on the past, not the present, but that may change."

Mary Ann looked up from her task. "How?"

Liz rested her hands on the counter, palms flat on the surface, facing the two other women. "Do either of you know Althea Mitchell well?"

Sadie and Mary Ann exchanged glances.

"I've talked to her on different occasions," Sadie said. "But we don't run in the same circles."

"Other than her friendship with Opal and knowing she's a Pleasant Creek resident," Mary Ann added, "I don't know her well."

Liz tapped a finger on the wood surface. "I got the impression that Althea is used to people being cowed by her credentials. Problem is, I showed up asking questions that will likely have a negative bearing on her family's reputation. At first, she acted like she didn't know a thing, but then I learned through Bert that Emma was married to her ancestor. Now, since I've been continuing my investigation despite her dismissal, I've found out she's already requested the same records that Julie just found. Why would she do that? What is she trying to hide?"

"Perhaps she unintentionally stumbled on Emma's spy story," Sadie reasoned.

"Which makes sense. But why did she initially pretend not to know about Emma? It couldn't have been a big surprise to her."

"To keep her research a secret, perhaps? Opal did say she's writing a paper. That would explain why she misled you."

A customer walked in, gazing around the showroom as if not sure where to begin shopping. Sadie left the group to wait on the woman.

Liz met Mary Ann's gaze. "What do you think?"

"Sadie's right. You've been so intent on finding out about Emma, you haven't given much thought as to whom it was that planted that bag with the letter and photo in your backyard. I'd say that's where you'll find your answers. It's probably the same person who left that note in the kitchen."

"But am I wrong in thinking Althea is hiding something?"

"Oh no, it sounds like that is a very real possibility."

Liz grinned. "Thanks. I was beginning to think I was the only one who found her behavior odd."

"While I may not know the woman, I do know she's proud of her family." Mary Ann paused. "Let's look at it from an opposite angle. What if in her research Althea came upon those very two items and placed them in your yard?"

Liz opened her mouth, closed it, and then opened it a second time. "Come again?"

"From her point of view, she doesn't want to add this new development to the family history she is writing."

"Because it changes everything."

"Yes," Mary Ann said. "The letter alone is somewhat unflattering, no matter what else comes to light. So Althea puts it somewhere strange, like near a bench in the yard of a busy inn, making sure to leave it apparent that someone had been digging there. With guests coming and going, someone's sure to find it."

"Makes sense in a sneaky kind of way."

"Once it's discovered, she can claim she knew nothing of Emma's past. Puts the blame elsewhere and keeps her reputation clean."

"What about the bones?"

Mary Ann looked stumped. "I don't know. Maybe the location she chose was just a coincidence."

"If you believe in that sort of thing." Liz tapped her chin. "If it *was* Althea who left the bag, she takes the heat off of herself with that move. Let the new resident in town, me, make her family history look sketchy. Who would believe me?"

"It's an angle you can't ignore."

"No. I suppose not." Liz sighed. "Still, no matter how Althea spins it, Emma has definitely cast a shadow over her family and put her in a tight spot."

Mary Ann folded a piece of fabric into a neat square. "What will you do next?"

Liz straightened her shoulders. "I think I'll have to talk to Althea again. It's time she met my alter ego, Lawyer Liz."

11

On Wednesday morning, after cleaning up the breakfast dishes, Liz dropped her errand list and a bottle of water into her sizable purse, grabbed her keys, and walked to the base of the stairs. Today was her big shopping day. It was time to replenish paper goods, cleaning supplies, and restock the refrigerator and pantry. She sighed as she thought about what was ahead. *Not exactly as fashionable as strolling down Newbury Street in Boston, window-shopping at upscale clothing stores or stopping at a trendy restaurant for lunch. Nope. Today I'll be walking up and down store aisles pushing an overflowing cart of supplies.*

"Sarah," she called up the stairs, "I'm leaving now."

Footsteps sounded above, and soon Sarah's head popped over the railing. "I am almost finished with the guest rooms."

"Great. I shouldn't be gone too long."

Liz stepped outside, accosted by the muggy air. In the last few days, the temperatures had steadily risen, making the days more humid. Unusual for this time of year, the thick air made it feel much hotter than the mercury reading on the gauge hanging on the porch.

She had the air-conditioning cranked high as she drove around town. Her rounds went smoothly, and soon she was checking items off her to-do list with a satisfying frequency. At her last stop, the pharmacy, she parallel-parked on Main Street and climbed out, heading toward the building with the big storefront windows and sale fliers taped to the door. She'd only taken a few steps when she noticed Althea Mitchell slumped on a shady bench beneath a nearby tree, absently fanning herself. Liz drew closer, disturbed by the woman's disheveled appearance. Despite the oppressive heat, her face was drawn and extremely pale.

Concerned, Liz marched her way. "Dr. Mitchell?"

Althea glanced up, her expression dazed. When she realized it was Liz, her eyes narrowed in anger, which soon faded, as if it took too much energy to maintain the emotion. "Liz."

"Are you feeling okay? It's awfully hot out today."

Shaking her head, Althea said in a subdued tone, "I'll be fine. Just waiting on Lesley to take me home."

Liz eased closer. "I can stay with you until she returns."

Althea shrugged. Liz took this as an invitation and settled on the bench beside her.

An uncomfortable silence ensued. Liz was about to make small talk when Althea cut into the silence. "I suppose you're still on the hunt to find out about Emma?"

Straight to the point. Liz hadn't intended on bringing up the subject of Emma since Althea looked so under the weather. "Perhaps right now isn't the best time to talk about her."

Althea sighed. "We don't have anything else in common."

"Maybe we do," Liz said.

"I doubt it, and I'm too tired to try and find out. So, proceed."

"Okay, then," Liz paused for a moment, "I do have a question for you. Did you plant the photo and letter on my property?"

"Did I what?" Althea's expression revealed confusion, not guilt.

"Let me back up. I came to you asking about Emma, and you weren't up front with me about your connection to her. I realize the letter puts what you know about your family history in a questionable light, and given your reputation, you might want to cover it up. So, theoretically, you planted the information at my place to put the validity of Emma's letter and her story in doubt. Your family reputation is safe."

"That's absurd," Althea sputtered, a splash of color staining her cheeks. "Yes, when I saw the picture of Emma with a man who wasn't my ancestor, it was a shock, but why on earth would I go to all the trouble of planting the picture with you?"

"Like I said, to save your reputation."

Peaked as she was, Althea sat up a little straighter. "Miss Eckardt, I have always been aboveboard. I'm not about to resort to dirty tricks now."

By the genuine look of affront in Althea's eyes, Liz believed her.

"All right. So how do you explain the brooch in the collection on your mantel? It's exactly the same as the one Emma has pinned to her dress in the picture."

Althea blinked. "What?"

"I've studied the photo with a magnifying glass—memorized it, actually. When I was at your house last time, I was admiring the jewelry and realized that one of the brooches in your possession is exactly like the one from the photograph."

Althea began to fan herself without much energy, as if her hand had become too heavy to raise. "That collection has been in the family for ages. It contains pieces from many of my ancestors."

Something about the woman's voice, so unsettled and lethargic, pinched at Liz's conscience. Althea seemed truly baffled by everything leading up to Liz finding the photo and letter. Could Liz just be reaching here? Wanting to make a connection? *Maybe.* Because if Althea knew nothing about the origin of the items, she couldn't have placed them on Liz's property. *But if she didn't plant anything, who did?*

"I'm sorry," Liz said. "I was only testing a theory, trying to get to the bottom of why the letter and photo were left on my property."

"I'm afraid I don't have an answer for you." Her face ghostly white again, Althea glanced over at the store. "What is keeping Lesley?"

"Can I get you anything? I have an unopened bottle of water in my purse."

"Please."

Liz fished out the bottle and opened it, handing it to Althea.

The older woman's hands trembled as she took the bottle and brought it to her lips. Her eyes closed after the first sip. "Thank you."

Liz had to admit she was getting worried. "Maybe we should get you to a doctor."

"I was there this morning. Lesley is getting my prescription."

Althea took another sip as Lesley exited the pharmacy. Her sunglasses covered her eyes, but Liz didn't miss the tightness of her jaw.

"What are you doing here?" Lesley asked once she'd reached the bench.

Liz stood. "I was running errands and stopped to talk with Althea."

"Dr. Mitchell isn't up for conversation." Lesley leaned down, face-to-face with her boss. "We should be getting home."

"Can I help?" Liz asked, swallowing the guilt that had her wishing she'd never come across the photo or letter.

Lesley shook her head. "I think you've done enough."

Althea rose with Lesley's help. The two women slowly moved to the car, Lesley holding Althea's arm to keep the older woman steady. Once Althea was seated inside the sedan, the younger woman rounded the car. She stopped beside the driver's door, facing Liz's direction. "Look, I know you're hot on the trail of finding out about the woman in the photograph, but you have to leave Dr. Mitchell out of it. She's under a lot of pressure right now and can't offer you any insight into the matter. She's not well. She's having trouble finishing her paper. Her family's reputation is at stake. Give her a break."

Liz shifted uncomfortably. Goodness. Had she caused Althea to come apart at the seams? "I didn't mean to—"

"Just leave her *alone*." Lesley opened the car door. "Please."

Standing alone on the sidewalk, Liz watched the car fade in the distance. She'd been positive Althea was behind all the activity pointing to Emma. Now, she wasn't sure.

"If you keep frowning like that you'll get wrinkles."

Liz turned to find Bert walking her way down the tree-lined sidewalk.

His gray hair looked extraordinarily fluffy this morning. Despite the sweltering heat, his shirt was ironed and his pants looked crisp. "Sorry, Liz, I couldn't resist. You looked so deep in thought."

Liz sighed. "I think I might have put too much pressure on Althea Mitchell. I asked her if she planted the photo and letter on my property."

"Well," Bert said in surprise, "I'm sure she didn't like the accusation."

"Especially since it's totally unsubstantiated. It was only a theory. She clearly had no idea what I was talking about."

"Althea likes the professional limelight too much to do anything underhanded."

"I get that now." Liz stared down Main Street. "She just looked so…ill."

Bert laid a hand on her shoulder. "Althea has had a few health issues these past years. I'm sure you didn't have anything to do with her physical state."

Liz wasn't so sure. "Tell that to Lesley. She warned me away from Althea."

"I don't know Lesley well, but I get the impression she's genuinely concerned with Althea's welfare. She's called me a time or two asking about historical records on Althea's behalf, and she's always been pleasant."

"Really? Does Althea call you when she needs information?"

"She has over the years. I believe I'm only one of her many sources."

That made sense. As she'd learned from Julie, it helped to have an active network of people in the field.

"How's your project coming along?" she asked.

Bert's face lit up. "I received the okay from the city council to get started. I intend to have an interactive display on the main floor of the building. I want visitors to know what we're all about here in Pleasant Creek."

"Sounds like fun."

"It should be, after I put in a lot of hard work." Bert paused. "I'm sorry that I haven't come up with anything for you just yet. Have you gotten any closer to finding out about Emma's activities?"

"A bit. I found another historian to work with. Julie Sonders. Do you know her?"

"I know of her." Bert looked down at the sidewalk, his tone guarded. "I've never had the occasion to speak to her personally, although Althea has mentioned her."

"Mentioned her in what way?"

Bert regarded her, his expression wary. "Althea warned me that Julie's out to make a name for herself in professional circles. She worried that Julie might take advantage of my generous nature."

"Because you love to share your knowledge?"

"Yes. Since Althea and I have known each other for years, we have a mutual respect and love of history. Althea felt that Julie might want to use any opportunity to get ahead without really paying her dues. Academic dues, that is."

This certainly wasn't news to Liz. Julie had made it more than clear she was hoping Liz's project would give her the credibility she sought.

"I don't think Althea needs to worry about Julie unseating her," Liz said. "Sure, Julie's hungry for recognition, but Althea is firmly grounded. Although, if what we suspect about her family history is true, there might be a few folks who will delight in the less-than-sterling revelations."

"My dear, first you have to prove Emma's acts were less than sterling. Right now she's possibly a war hero and a bride. Maybe the letter was misconstrued, or if not, John Ashby might have been an honorable man and had not sent her away even after learning the truth. Or maybe that photo was taken long before she ever met John. The Civil War changed many lives and not all for the better. Until you have evidence to the contrary, much more evidence than you have at this moment, you can't prove anything, and you shouldn't assume the worst."

"Thanks for reminding me of that."

He chuckled. "Finding historical facts is just about as time-consuming as police officers trying to track down clues to solve a crime, only far less dramatic. Speaking of the police, any news about your bony guest from the chief?"

"Nothing since he sent the bones off to the lab. I guess it'll depend on what they find. I know it takes time, but it's hard to be patient."

"In the meantime, I'll gather information about the Ashby clan. I told you they have deep roots in this area of Indiana, so once I've assembled a decent compilation of their history, I'll get it to you."

"I really appreciate it."

Bert grinned. "It's what I do."

Liz glanced at her watch. "I should finish my errands so I can get back to the inn. Guests are checking in later this afternoon, and I must be ready."

"Of course. If you have any questions, don't hesitate to ask. As I said, once I learn more about the Ashbys, you'll be the first to know."

As Liz and Bert parted ways, the image of Althea's wan face haunted Liz. As much as she wanted the truth behind the possible crime scene in her yard, it was time to leave Althea in peace and find the real culprit.

12

Liz returned to the inn on autopilot. She barely spoke as she and Sarah carried in the supplies and put everything away. Busywork always helped her think, so Liz set about the inn, delivering toiletries to the bathrooms, checking her computer for reservation requests, and figuring out which rooms to place future guests in.

As she tidied up the sitting room, a class finished at Sew Welcome. After the attendees had filed past and left through the front door, Liz went into the shop and found Mary Ann busy behind the counter while Sadie picked up after the class. Opal, at a table on the far side of the room, quietly folded her project.

Miriam glanced up from her task of packing up her supplies and smiled. "Hello, Liz."

"Looks like you were busy."

"Ja. I had a full class. I am very pleased with the students' choice of patterns."

Sadie sauntered over. "The quilt patterns are challenging, but this group of ladies is up for the job."

"You always say that if it were easy, anyone could do it," Mary Ann told Sadie.

"True, but I don't want it to be so difficult that we don't have repeat customers."

Everyone laughed, except for Opal. Just like the other night at the cupcake giveaway, Opal wouldn't meet Liz's gaze. Liz would have to make the first move.

With trepidation, she crossed the room to approach Opal. "Are you talking to me?"

"Only if necessary."

Liz almost smiled. Opal's dedication to Althea was admirable. And it made Liz realize that Opal was the kind of friend who would stand beside you, especially when things were tough. "For what it's worth, I am sorry for upsetting Althea. I didn't realize her health was so fragile. And I don't think she had anything to do with the bones or the photo and letter."

Opal met Liz's gaze, uncertainty lingering in the depths. "And I'm supposed to accept your word after the way you went about interrogating my friend?"

"No. But you should know I've apologized to her. Just a few hours ago, in fact. I was running errands and ran into her on Main Street."

"Odd. Althea told me she wasn't feeling well."

"She was waiting for her assistant outside the pharmacy. Althea said something about seeing the doctor and getting a prescription filled."

"Poor Althea. She hates to rely on anyone or anything, including doctors and medicine. She must truly be under the weather to willingly take a pill."

Liz nodded. "She didn't look well."

By this time, the other women had gathered around.

Opal placed the quilt in her tote. "I think she's been battling high blood pressure."

"Which stress doesn't help," Liz muttered.

Sadie laid a hand on her arm. "You can't blame yourself. You only asked questions. If Althea was less than forthright . . ." She shrugged.

"This entire situation is complicated," Liz said. "Althea admitted she knew about Emma the second time I visited her, but she didn't know anything about the brooch."

"Brooch?" Opal repeated.

"The one Emma is wearing in the photograph. There's one exactly like it displayed with other heirloom jewelry at Althea's house."

"You didn't tell us about the brooch," Mary Ann accused.

"Sorry. It's a recent development. Turns out it's a dead end anyway."

Mary Ann frowned. "Like the note?"

Sadie jumped on that piece of news. "What note?"

Liz ran a hand over her brow. "More complications." She blew out her cheeks and then explained about the note she'd found in her kitchen last week.

"Let me guess," Sadie said with more than a little irritation in her voice. "I bet the only reason Mary Ann brought it up is because she asked you to tell us and you didn't."

Chagrined, Liz smiled weakly at Sadie. "Busted."

"One moment." Miriam held up a hand. "Sarah told me about the envelope. She was very concerned that you were upset with her because someone had been in the kitchen."

"No. Of course not. Finding the letter concerned me, and I questioned Sarah about it, but that's it."

"She is worried because you have been acting strangely."

Liz glanced at Mary Ann. "You were right. I should have told everyone."

Sadie took Liz's hand. "My dear, we aren't trying to tell you what to do. We're concerned, for all involved. You, Althea, even our mysterious Emma."

"I know. And I appreciate you all more than I can say." Liz shook her head. "Ever since Beans dug up the bones, I've been on a mission. Only instead of getting answers, I seem to be upsetting everyone."

For the first time, a glimmer of a grin twitched Opal's lips. "I shouldn't have been so hard on you. Althea is difficult on a normal day, and I think we can all agree that these circumstances are not normal."

The other women nodded in agreement.

"So, what now, Liz?" Opal asked. "You don't suspect Althea of any wrongdoing?"

"It's clear the woman is genuinely upset and confused by what's happened. She was guilty of not telling me she knew about Emma, but now I'm sure she really doesn't have a clue about any of the events that have been going on."

"I'm glad that's established," Sadie said. "Let's get back to the brooch."

"Althea swears she knows nothing about it, that it's part of a collection of family heirlooms."

"Which is entirely possible," Opal said. "Between Althea, her husband, and their relatives, a lot of things end up at her house. One of the reasons she hired an assistant in the first place was to catalog their belongings. It's not a stretch that Althea wouldn't know she had something of importance to the Emma mystery."

"Lesley is in charge of cataloging?" This was news to Liz.

"As far as I know. Althea bought a new laptop for the job. She was excited to have a database of what they have accumulated over the years."

Liz's mind went into overdrive again. "I wonder what else Althea has at her house that might help us?"

"Liz," Opal warned, drawing out her name.

"You're right. I should leave Althea alone."

"But?" Sadie prompted, then chuckled.

"There is a pocket watch in the photo." The sensation that she was close to grasping something just outside her reach came over Liz. "If I could find out more about it, it might lead us to the identity of the man standing beside Emma."

A group of women walked into the store. Mary Ann told the ladies she'd be with them in a moment before saying to Liz, "You found a new historian to work with. Why don't you see what she can find out before you ask Althea again?"

"You're right. I don't want to bother Althea anymore unless it's absolutely necessary."

As the ladies went back to their tasks, Liz remained with Miriam.

"Is there something else, Liz?"

"I'm sorry if I made Sarah uncomfortable. I'll be sure to talk to her about it before she leaves today."

"This is one of the many lessons my daughter-in-law must learn as she goes through life."

"Yes, but she didn't do anything wrong." Liz closed her eyes for a moment. "I seem to be making a mess of things."

"But you can always make things right."

And she would. "Thank you, Miriam. And by the way, I started on my new quilt. I'd like you to look at it when we have a few free minutes. I'm not sure which stitching pattern I want to use once I finish the top."

"I would be honored."

They grinned at each other, relatives who would have never known each other if her mother's diary hadn't steered Liz to Pleasant Creek. Liz marveled once again at no longer being alone in the world, at not having to navigate life's travails solo, because now she had a family she could rely on within her reach. Feeling lighter than she had before coming into the store, Liz sought out Sarah. She found the young woman in the kitchen, wiping down the counter.

"Sarah. Good. I wanted to talk to you."

The young woman wiped her hands on the towel and straightened her apron, her face solemn when she asked, "Ms. Eckardt, have I done something wrong?"

"No." Liz took Sarah's hand and led her to the table. They both took a seat. "I'm afraid I've been so involved in the mystery behind the bones and the other items, I might have come across a bit intense for you."

Sarah managed a smile. "It is true, you are *misstrauisch*."

Liz raised an eyebrow.

"Suspicious," Sarah translated.

"Well, that's right on the money."

They both laughed.

"I wanted you to know that I appreciate your help," Liz said. "You certainly didn't sign up for all this craziness, but it's here all the same."

"I am glad we talked. I was not sure how to bring it up."

"Please, in the future, let me know if something is bothering you. I won't be the least bit offended. In fact, letting me know how you feel will make me a better boss. I'm still getting the hang of running the inn."

"I will tell you." The girl hesitated and then said, "I might know something."

Liz tilted her head. "Oh?"

"A few days before the bones were found, several phone calls came to the inn. When I answered, no one spoke and then the caller hung up. I did not think about it at the time, but could it be related to your mystery?"

"At this point anything is possible. Thank you for letting me know."

"I will head home now." Sarah stood. "The weekend is going to be busy. Would you like me to come in Saturday?"

"Yes, that would be a great help. Thank you, Sarah."

With a smile, Sarah departed. Liz sat at the table, staring out the window. The branches of a willow tree in the backyard swayed in the breeze. With all the humidity hanging in the air, were they in for more rain?

After a few moments, Liz rose and went to her room. She confirmed her guests' weekend reservations and jotted down some notes, but her mind wouldn't stay on the tasks at hand. Before long, she took out the copy of the photograph of Emma and the mystery man from the top drawer in her desk. Grabbing her magnifying glass, she examined the photo yet again. This time she focused on the pocket watch.

There wasn't much to go on. Only about half of it was visible, the rest nestled in the man's vest pocket. Along the edge a design had been etched into the metal. It was sort of a scroll image, but nothing distinctive.

Wait. That odd sensation tickled the back of her neck again. Hadn't there been a pocket watch similar to it displayed at Althea's house? *Okay, Liz, you're reaching here.* She'd really only given the other case a passing glance. Besides, the watch clearly belonged to the man in the photo, not Althea's family.

Liz pressed her lips together. She so wanted to know who this man was. He must have been important or why else would Emma have chanced having her picture taken with him? Liz had already determined he wasn't Emma's husband. So who was he? Someone she'd met while in the military? Someone she'd known before?

And then another idea hit her. If Emma had indeed been a spy infiltrating the Confederate army, she might have pretended to be involved with this man only to gain secrets from him. Maybe she'd posed for the photo at his request, maintaining a relationship with him to keep her cover. Certainly stranger things had happened.

"Who are you?" Liz whispered, not sure which of the figures she was addressing.

If Emma had been acting, if she was indeed undercover, then perhaps she had loved John Ashby after all and kept him in the dark because of war secrets. That would explain Althea's surprise.

Liz took out the copy of the letter and reread it. But why keep writing to F. when the war was over? Liz reasoned that if there had been no romantic entanglement, Emma could have let it go and have gone back to her life with no one else the wiser. Yet it seemed the opposite. Her own words told the story. Emma had kept up correspondence with the mystery man because she wanted to.

Liz sat back and sighed. Maybe Emma's story would be revealed in time. If Julie could find out more about Emma's activities during the war, it might answer all the questions raging through Liz's mind. With any luck, she might even be able to discover the identity of the man in the photo. Yes, it was a long shot, but it all came back to one simple fact.

Someone in Pleasant Creek wanted Liz to help Emma.

13

Early Friday afternoon, Liz met Julie at The Coffee Cup. The usually bubbly young woman greeted Liz with a solemn expression.

"I take it you haven't discovered much else about Emma?" Liz said by way of greeting.

"Unfortunately, no." Julie raised her hands, palms up in the air. "It's as though I've reached the end of the paper trail. And don't get me started on the man in the picture. He's like a ghost."

"So why did you call me for this meeting?" Liz took a sip of the latte she'd ordered.

"I want you to know where I stand. Plus, I need a plan of action to get Dr. Mitchell to hand over her information."

"I've already talked to Althea on the subject. For now, her expertise is off the table."

Confusion marred Julie's brow. "Why?"

Liz wasn't sure that Althea would want her health problems to be public information. "Let's just say that this is my decision for now."

Julie tapped a finger on the table. "Something tells me she knows more than she's saying."

"And if she does, it's okay." Another idea occurred to Liz. "Why don't you contact your friend Lesley? She's working for Althea. Maybe she can help."

"According to Lesley, so far all Dr. Mitchell lets her do is compile a list of her belongings."

"From what I understand, that's a big job."

"True, but Lesley was hoping to get more involved with Dr. Mitchell's writing," Julie said. "She's done some of the family research in the last two weeks but would love to play a larger role. Maybe work on a genealogy project. It doesn't sound like it's turning out that way."

"Maybe so, but Lesley takes good care of Althea."

"She's not a nursemaid." Julie's face went red at the idea of her friend being more of an aide than an assistant. "She's very smart."

Liz raised an eyebrow.

"Lesley's great at digging into ancestry files," Julie quickly added. "When she had a chance to interview to be an assistant for Dr. Mitchell, she jumped at the opportunity."

"Everyone has to pay their dues."

"She could pay her dues doing something she's good at." Julie shook her head as she turned her coffee cup round and round.

Liz read indecision there, as if Julie was building up to something. Instead of waiting her out, Liz cut to the chase. "Why don't you just tell me what's on your mind."

Julie sighed. "I'm concerned you might think I'm not doing a good job since I don't have any new leads for you."

"I understand that digging through documents and depending on different sources can be time-consuming. I'm impatient for news, but I know you're doing the best you can."

Relief washed over Julie's face. "I really am." As if bolstered now by Liz's words, she sat straighter in her chair. "I have an appointment next week with an old professor of mine. His area of expertise is the Civil War, so I'm hoping he can shed some light on this for us."

"See, you are on the job." Liz offered an encouraging smile. "Don't be so hard on yourself."

"This is my first major assignment since I left school. I want to find answers for you and hopefully let the academic world in on this new discovery."

"Just as long as I find out about Emma, I'm happy."

Julie glanced at her watch. "I need to get going. I have a few more stops to make this afternoon." She stood. "I'll call you after I speak to my professor."

Julie skirted the tables in the shop and stepped out into the bright sunshine. Her face lit up, and she waved at someone on the street out of Liz's view. Who had Julie spotted? A friend? A date, maybe?

Liz remembered her hectic schedule when she first started out after law school, balancing long hours at the firm with a busy social life. How exciting it had been when she first started dating her ex-boyfriend, Matt. She almost missed those days. Almost missed him. *But really, what could be more exciting than being an inn owner with old bones found buried on the property?* She answered her internal question with a quiet chuckle. At this point in her life, nothing could beat it.

Downing the remainder of her latte, Liz glanced at the time on her cell phone. Where had the last hour gone? She was about to rise when Jackson took a seat opposite her.

"Leaving already?" he asked with a disarming smile.

"I am." She grinned. "I have a few things to do back at the inn."

He nodded. As a businessman himself, he knew all about putting the job first. "Any news about your mysterious Emma?"

"We're kind of at a standstill. The historian I'm working with found more information than Althea gave us, but honestly, I'm not holding my breath."

"Throwing in the towel, are you?"

"Heavens no. Regrouping is more like it."

Jackson chuckled. "I heard Althea isn't taking the news of this woman's exploits well."

"No. Especially since we don't really know what Emma was up to. It could be nothing."

"Or it could be the key to everything."

Liz shrugged. "I wouldn't be surprised if Althea's having second thoughts about finishing the paper on her family history."

"She'll finish it. If only to keep up her reputation."

"I would have said the same thing a week ago, but now? I think this whole thing has taken a toll on her."

"Maybe I can be of some help," Jackson said. "If you have the time, that is."

Curious, she asked, "Are you secretly a historian?"

"No, but I ran into someone the other day who might be able to answer some of your questions."

Liz sat up straighter in her seat. "Go on."

"Her name is Clara Parks."

"That name sounds familiar."

"I believe she takes a quilting class at Sew Welcome."

That was it. Liz remembered Sadie talking about the one class that was a mixture of retirees and working women. "I think I waved to her last time she left the shop."

Jackson nodded. "She's a nice person. You'd like her."

"What's the connection?"

"The Parks family are longtime residents of Pleasant Creek. In fact, Clara's ancestors were servants for the wealthy Ashby family. When the Ashbys really started making money after the Civil War, they needed help to keep up the big house and grounds. Clara's family did so for generations."

"So, what you're saying is that if anyone has insider information, it's this woman."

"Exactly." He grinned sheepishly. "I should have thought of her sooner."

"I'm happy you remembered it now." Liz grew serious. "Do you think she'd talk to me?"

"As a matter of fact, I asked her that very question when I ran into her. At first she doubted you'd be interested in anything she might know, but then she decided she might have a story or two to tell about the Ashby clan."

Liz rose. "Then what are we waiting for?"

Jackson remained seated. "For her Friday afternoon bridge game to end. When I told her I was going to mention her family's connection to the Ashbys to you, she said we could come by later today, if you have time."

"I'll make the time." Liz grinned. "You really are a full-service mayor."

Jackson bowed in his seat. "I aim to please. Why don't I order us both another coffee while we wait? Then I can fill you in on my other good piece of news."

"Have you been holding out on me, Mayor?"

"I was afraid once I told you I had info, you'd steamroll right over me to get to the source."

"Am I that bad?"

"I happen to think persistence is a virtue."

She laughed. "At last, someone who appreciates me."

While Jackson talked to the barista, Liz called the inn to tell Sarah she'd be gone for a while longer. Then she quickly dialed Mary Ann.

"I have another lead."

"Besides your historian?" Mary Ann asked.

"Yes. Someone you know. Clara Parks."

"I love Clara. She's so sweet. Her husband passed away many years ago, and she's been alone ever since."

"You mean she was married, but she didn't change her last name?"

"Yes. That was unusual back then, but she'd made a promise to her father to keep her family name."

Liz let that tidbit of information sink in. "Do you think she's a good lead?"

"Probably."

"Since you know her, any suggestions on how to best approach her?"

"Just tell her what you've learned so far," Mary Ann said. "She's always been hush-hush about her family's relationship with the Ashbys, but she's downsizing and getting ready to move out of her home and into senior housing, so maybe you'll get lucky and strike pay dirt. Sometimes when people make big life changes and let go of belongings, they let go of the old secrets attached to them."

"It certainly can't hurt to have another source of information."

Jackson approached the table holding two cups of coffee, and Liz wrapped up her conversation with Mary Ann.

"Notifying the rumor mill?" Jackson asked.

"If Mary Ann's part of it, then yes."

"Mary Ann, maybe. Sadie, for sure."

Liz laughed. "What can I say? They're curious."

"Don't I know it. I've lived here a long time, remember?"

Liz hid her smile behind a sip of her beverage. After swallowing the delicious mocha latte, she asked, "So, what's the second piece of good news you have for me?"

"I ran into Bert earlier this morning. He's tracking down a new avenue of research, but until he finds anything pertinent to the Emma story, he's reluctant to say much. Most likely he doesn't want to let you down."

"Bert is so sweet. I'm glad he's on my side."

"Given enough time, he'll sniff out a story. History is his passion, so if he's onto something, expect results."

"That's good to know." Liz took another sip and studied Jackson. The mayor of Pleasant Creek was a genuinely nice man, not to mention incredibly handsome. Since she'd agreed to go to the awards banquet with him, why not use this opportunity to get to know him better? "So what about you? What are you passionate about?"

Jackson leaned back in his chair and replied so quickly that it was evident he didn't need to think about his answer. "I love this town, and I love making furniture. Guess that would be it in a nutshell."

"Admirable."

"My dad never had to worry about me not wanting to follow in his footsteps. He loved the furniture business and was excited to hand it over to me."

"A family legacy. There's something to be said about the timelessness of tradition. As the years go by, I find it a comfort to hold on to."

"Will the Olde Mansion Inn become your legacy?"

Liz smiled, liking the sound. "I hope so, although I'm not sure my godson, Steve, has an interest in small-town innkeeping."

"Here's a tip I've learned about being in business. Keep investing parts of yourself into what you love, and your legacy will last for generations. I'd say the Olde Mansion Inn is in good hands."

"Thank you for the vote of confidence." She wrinkled her nose. "I don't want unknown bones found on the property to be forever associated with the inn."

"You don't think the story would look good on the official inn website?"

"Hardly."

He held up his cup as if in a toast. "Then I guess you'll have to get to the bottom of it."

Liz raised her cup in return. "Here's to solving the mystery."

They continued to sip their coffees until Jackson's phone dinged. He took a look and smiled. "That's Clara. She's home now."

"You text with her?"

"We exchanged numbers when she made the invitation. The woman has skills."

Liz laughed as she rose.

Jackson stood and pushed in his chair. "After you."

"Thanks. And you might note that despite my overwhelming curiosity, I'm not racing you to the car to see who can get there first. I'm taking my time. When we get there, we get there."

"I know it's killing you."

"Yes, but look how well I hide it."

Jackson held the door open for her. "C'mon before the excitement gets the better of you."

Liz pulled her car keys from her purse. "Should I follow you?"

"Why don't I just drive?"

Liz dropped her keys into her purse. "Lead on."

Jackson strode to his pickup truck and opened the passenger door for her. "Hope you don't mind riding in the work truck. My car is at home." He pushed some papers into the center console and brushed off the seat.

"I don't mind at all," she said, climbing inside. It had been years since she'd traveled in a pickup. Unlike her sleek Acura sedan, the cab was roomy and high off the ground, giving her a better perspective of her surroundings. Liz could see why people liked driving trucks.

"Clara lives a few minutes out of town," Jackson said as he jumped in. "It won't take long to get there."

He started the truck and pulled into Main Street traffic. As they made their way out of town, Liz lowered her window, letting the warm breeze blow through her hair.

They whizzed along, and she admired the landscape, so different from Boston. They passed acres of farmland, some tilled and some already planted. Liz loved the creeks that meandered through the countryside, a splash of color in the otherwise repetitive beige and brown soil of future corn and soybean fields.

She saw a group of men wearing straw hats to combat the sun as they worked on a barn. Half a dozen children ran through the grass nearby. They passed some of the farmhouses, and Liz noticed gardens in the yards. Maybe next year she'd plant some vegetables.

Even with Kiera's help, it had been a massive project to spruce up the inn grounds since Liz took ownership of the inn. Now with tourist season nearing its peak, she'd have to put off any time-consuming activities. Her guests kept her busy enough.

Before long, Jackson turned the pickup into a gravel driveway leading to a two-story farmhouse.

"This is it. The house has been in Clara's family for generations."

A For Sale sign with a Sold sticker placed on it sat at the edge of the yard. The grass was slightly overgrown, but it was nothing that a good mowing wouldn't put right. As she walked up the brick path to the porch, Liz saw that the flower beds were neglected, and the house could use a fresh coat of paint. Despite the run-down appearance, someone had seen the potential in the place. It had good bones and was ideal for a growing family to spread out and enjoy the land.

Liz rang the doorbell.

Before long, a woman with neatly styled gray hair and dark-rimmed glasses opened the door. She blinked at Liz, but a smile spread across her lips as her gaze moved to Jackson. "Mayor Cross. Hello."

"Hello to you too, Clara." He glanced at Liz. "This is my friend Liz Eckardt. She'd like to learn more about the Ashby family."

"Indeed. It is a story to tell."

Liz stepped forward. "I'm intrigued."

Clara opened the door wider. "I hope you still feel the same way when you leave."

14

"Please, come inside," Clara Parks said as she waved Liz and Jackson into the front hall.

Liz's stomach danced with nerves, especially after Clara's cryptic statement. It might be her imagination, but the older woman's solemn expression seemed to imply she had something big to tell them. But if Liz had learned anything the past few days, it was to tread lightly. She wouldn't make the same mistake of approaching this woman the way she had Althea.

"Are you sure it's okay? We aren't prying?"

"I wouldn't have invited you if I felt that way." Clara led them to a cheerful living room. "Have a seat."

As Liz lowered herself to the faded couch, she moved a neatly folded quilt out of the way. Her fingers brushed the soft material. Homemade. Worn. As if it had been lovingly used through good times and bad.

"Your creation?" she asked Clara.

"I made it many years ago. I still keep up with the craft, so I have to thank you for reopening the inn. I missed spending time at Sew Welcome." Clara took a seat in a well-worn armchair. "I'm taking Miriam Borkholder's class. She's teaching me things I never knew how to do, and she does it all with that old-fashioned machine."

"Miriam's a great talent." Pride filled Liz. She knew Miriam's class would be a hit.

Jackson asked Clara about an acquaintance, and Liz took the opportunity to take in her surroundings. She made a mental comparison to Dr. Mitchell's house. In contrast, Clara's modest home had a welcoming air that Althea's stately residence lacked. Family pictures were scattered about the room, and there wasn't a collection of anything in sight. Sealed moving boxes were stacked in one corner, and an open box stood on the floor next to a half-empty bookshelf.

Clara caught Liz's scan of the room. "Don't mind the mess. I'll be moving soon."

"Where to?" Jackson asked.

"Pleasant Creek Retirement Community. It's gotten to be too much to take care of this house on my own. I don't even putter in the yard anymore. It's time to downsize and enjoy my golden years instead of slaving away here."

"Smart idea."

Clara's wistful gaze caressed the room. "It's time some other family started making memories in this old house." Clara turned back to Liz. "I understand you're seeking information. How can I help?"

"I'm hoping you can tell me about Emma Ashby. I haven't been able to find out much about her."

"She caused quite an uproar in the Ashby family," Clara said with a twinkle in her eye. "That's for sure."

"In what way?"

"First, by becoming involved with the military during the Civil War. Of course, the family didn't learn of Emma's secret enlistment until after the war. As far as the Ashbys were concerned, proper ladies helped with the war effort from a safe distance."

"But Emma decided otherwise."

Clara nodded. "She was very independent. Spoke her mind. John's parents were not happy when they learned the truth, but Emma was an heiress, and they needed a cash infusion. There was money to be made then, but only for those who could invest. The Ashbys didn't dare risk offending Emma for fear she would take her inherited fortune and leave before the wedding. Emma and John had gotten engaged just before the war broke out, but then she went back East for the duration. They didn't want her to, but they had no control over her actions."

"What about her own family?"

"The Hartsfelds were an influential family at the time. Unfortunately, she doesn't mention them much in her writings."

Liz felt her mouth gape as her excitement doubled. "She has writings?"

Jackson looked at Liz and chuckled. "You look like a little kid on Christmas morning."

Liz felt that way too. Maybe she'd finally caught a break. Clara might actually be able to lead them to the truth about Emma.

"Emma kept a journal," Clara said. "My family's held on to it all these years."

This news left Liz completely speechless—for a moment. Then the full implication of Clara's words clicked in Liz's brain. "A journal Althea doesn't know about?"

"Correct."

"And you never told her?"

Clara's eyes sparkled in affirmation.

"But why keep it a secret?"

"It's a long story. Just as the Ashby family has a legacy, so does the Parks family," Clara said. "As members of the household staff, the Parkses kept the Ashbys' secrets up until the 1940s. By then the Ashby family numbers had dwindled, as had their fortune. They downsized and didn't need domestic help. My parents were the last to be employed by the Ashbys. And the last to keep their secrets. They called keeping those confidences 'guarding their secret vow.' All very mysterious."

"What was the vow?"

"I can't say, really. You see, once my parents stopped working for the Ashbys, the vow ended with them."

"And the journal?" Jackson prompted.

"I recently found it in a box when I was cleaning out the attic. It had been hidden there for years. I'm not sure if my folks forgot about it or not. Anyway, I read the journal, and that's how I came to know about Emma."

"Is there any chance I could see the journal?" Liz spoke in as calm a voice as she could muster. She felt like she wanted to leap across the room and whoop for joy.

"Before I give you an answer, you must know that I have given this considerable thought. I wondered if it was right to let anyone else read the book or if I should just destroy it in honor of 'the vow.' I'm not entirely sure why the previous Parkses kept the journal from the Ashbys. I can only assume Emma had a special relationship with one of my ancestors and confided a secret she'd kept from her husband."

"This all seems very serious," Liz said.

"To my family, it was."

"And now?"

Clara met Liz's gaze head-on. "Now I determine if you're the one to help Emma."

Help Emma? Liz shivered. Was it a coincidence that she used the same wording that was written on the note left at the inn?

"Finding those bones on your property must have been an unsettling experience," Clara continued, "and now you're asking about Emma. Do you believe there's a connection?"

"The photograph, the letter, and the bones all in one place? I don't think it can be random."

"I must choose wisely who I'll entrust her story to."

Liz scooted to the end of the cushion. "I know I haven't been in Pleasant Creek very long, but please know I would never do anything underhanded in searching for or revealing the truth."

Letting out a long sigh, Clara gripped the armrests of the chair. "People aren't going to be happy about the truth."

"Althea, you mean."

Clara nodded. "And I can't say I blame her. She's lived large on her family's good standing. Once the truth comes out, things are going to change."

If Althea's state of health was any indication, the historian already had an inkling that things weren't roses and perfection in the Ashby family history. Althea might not have known about the journal, but once she did, would she want it destroyed?

"If you wish," Liz said, "I'll keep anything you tell me confidential."

"I think the time for secrets is over, but thank you for offering." Clara smiled. "Sadie and Mary Ann admire you. I trust their judgment, so I choose to trust you."

"And I can vouch for her as well," Jackson said, his serious expression so at odds with his usually playful demeanor.

Liz's chest grew tight. The people in this town meant so much to her. They had accepted her as one of their own. She silently thanked her mother again for pointing her in the direction of Pleasant Creek.

Clara rose from her seat. "Excuse me for just a moment."

Once she left the room, Liz turned to Jackson. "I have a feeling Emma's story is a doozy."

"I have to admit, even I'm more than a little curious now."

After a few minutes, Liz noticed the steady tapping of her foot. She placed a hand on her thigh to keep it still. She couldn't remember ever being this enthralled, even when she was knee-deep in law cases that kept her absorbed for weeks.

Clara returned, a small box in her hands. She set it on the coffee table, pulled back the flaps, and removed a book. The leather cover and binding were wrinkled and discolored with age. On the bottom left corner of the smooth leather cover, *EHA* was written in neat cursive. Emma's handwriting. Liz recognized it from the old letter.

Clara handed the journal to Liz. "Take it."

Liz took the book reverently, running her fingers over the well-worn surface. What answers would she find here? Liz opened the cover, smiling when she read aloud, "This journal belongs to Emma Hartsfeld Ashby." The paper was coarse, the edges uneven. As she flipped through the pages, Liz noticed some words were heavy with ink, others lighter, as if the ink had dried differently depending on the mood of the person wielding the pen. But the handwriting was unmistakably Emma's.

This was so much more than Liz had expected.

"If you're like me," Clara said, "you'll probably want to read it in private. Savor each word. I know I did just that when I found it."

Liz's head jerked up. "You're letting me keep it?"

Clara shrugged. "Like I said, I won't have much room when I move. After you read through the journal and sort through the new information, we'll figure out what to do next."

Liz rested her hand over the cover. "I'm honored."

"Just do Emma proud."

Again, Clara's words puzzled her. "You wouldn't by any chance be the mystery person who left the photo and letter on my property? Or the note in my kitchen?"

"Why would I do that?"

Why, indeed? Clara wasn't saying yes, but she wasn't saying no either.

"You can take the box too," Clara said. "There are some old photos in there you might enjoy viewing."

Jackson crossed to the table and lifted the box. "We should probably be going."

"Yes." Liz stood. "I need to get back to the inn. The guests like it when I greet them at check-in."

Clara walked them to the door. On impulse, Liz hugged her. When she pulled back, the older woman smiled at her, sheer pleasure in her eyes.

"Don't be a stranger," Clara urged.

Liz waved goodbye as she walked to the truck. Once settled inside, she angled in the seat to face Jackson. "I don't know what to say, except thank you."

Jackson started the engine. "My pleasure. Like you said, I'm a full-service mayor. But I would appreciate a debriefing once you've read the journal."

"Of course."

As they drove back to town, Liz ran her fingers over the journal again, anxious for some quiet time so she could learn more about Emma. The Material Girls would flip when she showed them the journal. Althea's reaction, however, was going to be a different story.

"You know," Liz said slowly, "I feel kind of bad for Althea. This book could change everything she knows about her family, and she doesn't even know it exists."

"Your world wasn't the only one rocked when those bones were discovered."

"Very true."

Jackson pulled onto Main Street, then drove toward Liz's car.

Just before she got out of the truck she said, "If protecting Emma's secret ended with Clara's folks, I wonder what their vow was."

Jackson stared out the windshield for a few beats before his hooded eyes met hers. "I don't know, but I'd wager this story is far from over."

———

Liz hurried through the front door of the inn, hoping she'd made it back before her guests arrived. Sarah walked into the foyer, her face lighting up when she saw her boss.

"I thought I might have to greet our guests, but not one has arrived yet."

"Thank you, Sarah. I'll put my things in my room and help you get ready."

After depositing her purse on her desk, she placed the journal inside the top drawer and decided to lock it. Better safe than sorry. She hurried to the kitchen to find Sarah placing freshly baked cookies on a decorative plate.

"Is the tea made?"

"Ja. Everything is ready to be placed out."

"Excellent. Anything going on that I should know about?"

"You had some calls. I wrote down the information."

Liz took over cookie duty while Sarah went to get the messages.

"There were a few inquiries regarding the inn," Sarah read as she came back into the kitchen. "Also a call from Julie Sonders." She was the very woman Liz did not wish to speak with at the moment. Liz wanted to reflect more on her visit with Clara and read the journal first. "Julie asked you to call her back as soon as possible."

Liz nodded. "That'll have to wait. We're ready for check-in."

As she went to the foyer, a couple from Chicago, Mr. and Mrs. Booth, walked through the front door, raving about the inn's charm. Liz took their information and showed them to the Heirloom Room, just as Mrs. Booth had requested when she called to make reservations. The pretty middle-aged woman gushed over the four-poster bed while Mr. Booth munched on oatmeal cookies.

When Liz went back downstairs, two sisters who had made reservations were waiting for her, chatting with Sarah, asking her about her Amish lifestyle. Liz took them to the Rose of Sharon Room, answering more of their questions. They loved the vintage furniture and asked if there was a local store where they could buy reproductions. Naturally, Liz mentioned Cross Furniture Company. The sisters were discussing their shopping strategy when Liz ducked out.

Much later, after Sew Welcome closed and the inn was settled down for the night, Jackson's parting words rang in Liz's ears.

This story is far from over.

When Liz finally closed the door to her quarters for the night, she pounced on the journal and pored over Emma's words.

As Liz had suspected, Emma did have a love interest. But even in her private journal, she continued to refer to him only as F. After reading about the Ashbys, Liz understood why.

By her own admission, Emma was afraid for her life. She never said who threatened her, but Liz had her suspicions. Until she found out more about the Ashby family, she couldn't prove anything though.

She'd touch base with her connections and maybe together they'd figure it out. There was no point upsetting Althea and making things more difficult for her.

Emma had had secrets and worries—legitimate worries. After reading the final entries, Liz had to admit *she* was concerned for the safety of this woman who had lived and died almost a century and a half ago.

Exhausted, Liz rested the book on her stomach, her eyelids drooping. She'd just nodded off when the journal slipped from her stomach, slid down the bedspread, and fell to the hardwood floor with a thud. Liz jumped, and then blinked, realizing the book had fallen. She reached over the side of the bed to retrieve it, but her fingers couldn't snag the leather cover. With a sigh, she slipped from the sheets and knelt down on the floor.

As Liz picked up the journal, she noticed the leather had come loose on the back side. *Oh great. I hope I didn't ruin it.* What had she been thinking? She needed to take better care of the old book that had been entrusted to her.

She climbed back on the bed and placed the journal on the covers, gently inspecting the damage to the back of the book. The lining tucked under the leather binding had come apart. As she examined it more closely, Liz noticed something tucked inside the two pieces. Carefully, she removed a piece of paper.

Only it wasn't paper. It was another photograph, a portrait of a man. The same man in the first photo with Emma, the man Liz only knew as F, looked back at her. In this shot, his eyes still held the twinkle of merriment Liz had noted before. Even in the low lighting of her bedside lamp, she realized he was quite handsome. No wonder Emma had been taken with him.

Turning the picture over, Liz gasped. In neat capital lettering was written the name she had been searching for since the day she found the first photo.

Emma's mystery man was no longer a mystery.

15

The next morning Liz called Julie and blurted out the name of the man in the picture: Frederick P. Hardy. She asked for any information Julie could dig up on him, and they agreed to meet later at the inn to compare notes. Next, Liz left Bert a message to share the news. Finally, Liz called Mary Ann to see if the Material Girls were planning to meet that night to work on their projects. Liz couldn't wait to bring her friends up to speed.

The day dragged on as Liz completed tasks around the inn. The refrigerator was acting funny, so she called for service, and a toilet needed to be unplugged upstairs. As she cleaned up after taking care of the problem, she had to grin. *Ah, the glamorous life of an inn owner.* But the inn was hers, so she didn't mind dealing with the messy jobs. Someone had to do it.

In the middle of her busy day, she decided to try a new recipe. *A soufflé might jazz up the breakfast routine.* When the oven bell rang, Liz pulled out her newest experiment, frowning at the concave center. The rim had turned darker than it was supposed to. She held it up next to the picture in the cookbook she'd gotten the recipe from.

"No resemblance," she told her employee as they surveyed the sorry state of the sunken concoction that had come out of the oven.

Sarah laughed at the failed soufflé.

"Do you want a bite?" Liz offered the dish to Sarah, making her laugh harder.

Liz dumped the mess in the trash. She would have considered it a disaster, but she'd never seen Sarah laugh so hard.

Julie called mid-afternoon to say she had news. By the excitement in her voice, Liz suspected the young woman had a lead. She invited

Julie to meet with the Material Girls later that evening, so they could compare notes and tell Emma's story all at one time.

Then Liz dealt with a guest who didn't like the brand of soap she supplied in the bathrooms, returned phone calls, and set out the afternoon cookies for her guests. By the time she arrived, slightly late, at Sew Welcome, she was drained.

"Sorry," Liz said as she entered the shop, her arms full of her quilt project and Emma's journal. "Just in case you were wondering, innkeeping isn't as glamorous as you might think."

"Take a seat," Sadie ordered, "and a deep breath."

Caitlyn nearly bounced in her seat. "I've been working overtime and looking forward to getting together with you girls for days." She shot Liz a glance. "You'd better have an update."

"I do." Liz took her own seat and grinned at the expectant faces looking her way. "Emma kept a journal."

Silence fell for five seconds before simultaneous questions bounded her way.

Liz held up a hand. "One at a time."

Mary Ann's hand shot up. "Start at the beginning."

"That's not a question," Naomi teased.

"But a very reasonable suggestion," Opal said.

Liz began by telling them about Jackson's suggestion to visit Clara Parks, their trip to her home, and the revelation about Emma's journal.

"Apparently the Parks family had some secrets the Ashbys didn't know about." Liz held up the book for the group to see. "This being one of them."

"Did you read it?" Naomi asked.

Liz nodded. "Twice through."

Before Liz had a chance to continue, Julie rushed in. "Sorry I'm late." She glanced around the group. "Did I miss anything?"

"Liz was just starting to tell us about the journal," Sadie said as she pulled another chair closer to the group and motioned for Julie to take a seat.

"You go first," Julie told Liz. "I'll fill in after."

All eyes turned to Liz.

"Emma was betrothed to John Ashby before the Civil War broke out. She didn't really say how she felt about being engaged. She wrote about duty and requirement. Since she was an heiress from a wealthy family, I'm wondering if it was arranged. She didn't seem to be very excited at the prospect of marrying John Ashby.

"Once John left for war, the town got involved with the war effort, but Emma decided to do more than cook and give supplies to the soldiers. She chose to enlist."

"Which women could not do back then," Julie interjected. "Many women volunteered for the war effort, mostly as nurses and relief workers, but there were those who were secret soldiers."

"How could she have just up and left?" Mary Ann asked. "I don't imagine women traveled on their own back then."

"She told the Ashbys she was returning to her family back East during the war. I don't know if she actually did that or if it was just her cover story. Whatever the case, it allowed her to leave for a long period of time without arousing suspicion from the Ashbys."

"Obviously they believed her if she left town," Sadie said, "but where did she go?"

"Since women weren't allowed to enlist, some got around it by disguising themselves as men and changing their names. Julie and I already discovered that Emma went by E. Hartsfeld."

"I like this woman already," Caitlyn said as she added a few more stitches to a lovely quilt of yellow, green, and blue fabric. The Material Girls were making quilts to donate to the neonatal unit of the local hospital.

Liz continued, "While most female spies got their information from dinner parties or other social events, Emma disguised herself as a man and worked in a military camp. While she was there, she met a Confederate prisoner whom she fondly refers to in her writings as F."

"Frederick Percy Hardy." Julie said.

Sadie clasped her hands together. "How exciting!"

"There's more," Liz said. "Somehow he discovered her true identity. She writes that they talked for hours and quickly fell in love. She eventually helped him escape and disguised herself once again to travel with him. She says they were making their way to his home south of Atlanta."

Julie pulled her notes from her briefcase. "Correct. Macon, Georgia, to be exact. The Hardy family still resides there today."

"So what happened when they got there?" Naomi asked, her quilting project forgotten in her lap, as they were all drawn into the story.

"They didn't get there," Julie said. "Along the way they came upon a camp of deserters—desperate starving men. They were separated, and Emma later learned Frederick was killed in the skirmish."

Opal's hand flew to her throat. "How awful."

"Heartbroken, she made her way back to Indiana, keeping the truth of her travels a secret, and continued to help at home until the war ended. John returned a hero from his own service, and they married as planned. But here's the kicker. About a year later, Frederick showed up on Emma's doorstep."

Naomi gasped as the rest of the women stared at Liz with wide eyes.

"I *knew* he wasn't dead," Sadie added with a sniff.

Caitlyn scooted to the edge of her seat. "What did she do?"

Liz ran a hand over the leather cover of the journal. "I have to say, it was wrenching to read. After falling into each other's arms again, and Emma marveling that Frederick was alive, they had to face reality. Emma felt she couldn't leave John, and Frederick didn't want to sully her reputation, so he left."

"This is better than a romance novel," Caitlyn said in a hushed voice.

"A real tearjerker." Opal wiped at her eyes.

"In the journal, Emma writes that she and Frederick exchanged letters until she decided it was too dangerous. The letter I found in the bag was her last correspondence."

"Wait," Caitlyn interjected. "Why didn't Frederick have the letter if it was the last one she wrote to him?"

"Another part of the mystery."

"Which I can solve," Julie said with a satisfied smile. "But you first, Liz."

Liz swallowed hard and delivered the last piece of news. "In her journal, Emma swore that Frederick was her one true love."

After a prolonged silence, Sadie stood. "I don't know about you, but I need a bracing cup of tea. Liz?"

Everyone agreed, and the group headed to the kitchen.

Naomi held up a foil-covered dish. "I brought some pastries and cookies from the bakery. I'll put them out in the dining room."

Caitlyn grabbed plates, forks, and napkins. Mary Ann collected tea bags from the pantry while Liz set the kettle to boil. Opal got out the cups, and Julie helped carry them to the table. Sadie stood on the sidelines of the action, calling out orders like a master sergeant.

Once the ladies were settled around the dining room table, Liz nodded to Julie. "You're up."

Julie preened for a moment, making a show of organizing her papers. "Once Liz called me with the gentleman's name, I was able to locate the Hardy family. They still live in Georgia. I hope you don't mind, Liz, but I took the liberty of calling a member of the family."

"Not at all. I'm glad you took the initiative."

Julie grinned. "Let's hope the readers of my paper will agree." She smiled at the women, her face earnest when she said, "I'm hoping this will be a big career booster for me."

"We hope so too," Mary Ann said charitably.

"I spoke to Peter Cummings, a descendant of the Hardy clan. He keeps the family history and was very well informed. We spoke for a good hour."

Caitlyn made a rolling motion with her hand, as if to say "get on with it."

Julie cleared her throat, for dramatic effect Liz surmised. "The entire Hardy family knew about Frederick and Emma. And unlike Dr. Mitchell, Peter was more than happy to talk about it."

Liz chanced a glance at Opal, but her friend kept an even expression on her face.

"When Frederick came home after locating Emma, he was heartbroken. He never married and always insisted Emma was his one and only love."

Naomi picked up one of her cookies, but instead of taking a bite, she crumbled the edges. "How sad."

"It is. But here's the twist." Julie straightened her shoulders. "According to Hardy family lore, Frederick was worried about Emma when he returned home. He couldn't shake the bad feeling, so against his family's advice, six months later he returned to Pleasant Creek."

"He came back?" Liz asked, taken by surprise.

"Yes. And apparently at the second visit she was pale and very sickly. She insisted she'd caught some kind of fever and was having a hard time getting better, but she assured him she would eventually be fine. Reluctantly, Frederick returned to Macon. By year's end, Emma had passed away."

Sadie placed her teacup on its saucer. "A double heartbreak for that poor man."

"Yes. He came home absolutely convinced that John Ashby had done something to Emma to make her sick, but he could never prove it."

Caitlyn scoffed. "Because she didn't look good when he last saw her? Kind of a leap, don't you think?"

"Perhaps he knew deep down inside that something was wrong." Sadie was a staunch proponent of intuition—and conspiracy theories.

"He might have wanted to take Emma to a doctor, but in light of their relationship, I doubt she would have let him." Julie dipped her tea bag in the hot water. "Besides, there were still many illnesses medicine didn't cure back then."

"She might even have gotten sick when she was traveling," Opal surmised. "Conditions couldn't have been very sanitary back then."

"Whatever the truth of her health was, we don't know for sure." Julie leaned her elbows on the table. "According to Peter, Frederick believed that Ashby money could silence anyone who knew the truth, whatever that truth was. He felt that the accusations of a heartbroken and possibly bitter Southerner would go unheeded. Emma had married another man, after all.

"After his visit, Emma didn't want to exchange any more correspondence. By her letter, we know she was afraid of something. She wrote one last time, but obviously that letter was never delivered."

"But why would John hurt Emma?" Opal asked. "Althea said they had an uneventful marriage."

"Unless he found out the truth about his wife and another man," Liz speculated. "I'm not saying he did anything as horrible as killing his wife, but if he found out about Frederick, he wouldn't have been happy."

"And the Ashbys wouldn't have liked having a scandal attached to their prominent family name," Mary Ann concluded.

"If there was a secret in the Ashby family, Althea must have known about it and covered it up," Julie said with a smug curve of her lips.

"I don't know." Liz lightly tapped her spoon on the table. "She seemed genuinely ignorant about this part of her family history. I think she's as bewildered as we are."

"Then what about Clara?" Opal reminded them. "She must know more than she's saying."

"I didn't get that impression," Liz told her. "But that doesn't mean anything. This story gets more convoluted as we go along."

"Perhaps we'll never know the truth," Naomi commented.

"Well, I intend to keep searching," Julie announced as she collected her notes. She caught Liz's eye. "Are you still in this with me?"

More like the other way around, Liz thought, but she understood. "Yes. There's got to be some more information out there."

Julie shoved her papers in her satchel and shouldered the bag. "How about I come back tomorrow, and we can work on it together?"

"Sounds good. About one?"

"I'll be here." Julie looked around the table. "Thank you for including me. I appreciate your time and the delicious snack." She smiled at Naomi. "I'll definitely be visiting Sweet Everything soon."

After she left, Liz let out a long breath. "Wow. What a night."

Opal glanced at her watch. "And past time to get home. George will be worried."

The ladies carried the dishes and cups into the kitchen, pitching in until cleanup was finished. Then they trooped back to Sew Welcome to retrieve their projects. It was close to midnight when Mary Ann turned off the lights in the shop.

"Beans's discovery has turned into a major deal," she remarked.

"Never in a million years did I think I'd run into this kind of situation when I bought the inn."

"Try to get some sleep," Mary Ann advised as she slipped out the front door.

"You too."

Liz turned off the lights and was just about to go to her room when a light rapping sounded at the door to the four-season room off the kitchen. Her stomach dipped. Who would be calling this late at night? And why would they use the back door?

Liz flipped on the light, walked across the four-season room, and looked outside. Opal stood there lifting her hand to knock again.

Liz pulled the door open. "Opal. Did you forget something?"

"No. I wanted to speak to you. Alone."

"Come in."

Liz motioned to the chairs, but Opal shook her head.

"This will only take a moment," she said.

"What's so important that you snuck around to the back door?"

Opal looked everywhere but at Liz. "I'm afraid Althea wasn't quite as up front as we thought."

"Pardon?"

"A few weeks ago she mentioned that she had a lead on some family history she hadn't known about before. She was excited and thinking about writing another paper once she had all the details."

"You think she knew more about Emma than she let on?"

"No. I think she had no idea of the depth of Emma's story. Just like us."

"So . . .?"

"So I'm worried about Althea. She hasn't returned my calls. Her assistant is no help." Opal swallowed hard. "Do you think she had anything to do with the bones?"

"Althea would have had to know they were buried here, but the discovery seemed to come as a surprise to everyone." Liz shivered in the dim lighting as she remembered the modern plastic bag found with the old bones. "Or did it?"

16

Monday afternoon, Liz took another sip of her now cold coffee, grimacing at the bitter taste. Time had escaped her as she and Julie pored over the journal and Julie's research, looking for clues about Emma's life and who might have left the picture and letter. Even though she kept her suspicions to herself, Liz had a pretty good idea who it was. Why this person wasn't forthright about it was another story, but Liz wouldn't point fingers without first gathering all the evidence that was necessary to prove her assumptions.

"The more I think about it," Liz said, "the more I'm concerned about Emma's last days. Her writing in the last section of the journal seems a bit ominous, don't you think?"

Julie shook her head. "Although she doesn't mention Frederick's second visit—which is in itself strange—if you look at the dates, from around that time on, her penmanship is sloppy, and her thoughts are jumbled. Before then she was very concise and honest about her emotions."

"But even with her confused writing, I got the feeling she was frightened. Listen to this." Liz opened a page she'd flagged earlier and read aloud, "'I must be brave in these last hours.' Also, 'I cannot face those who would hurt me.'"

"I noticed that too."

"I think she knew whatever had made her ill was killing her."

"An illness with an origin that has never been revealed." Julie grabbed a paper from her stack. "What if Frederick was right and there was something suspicious going on?"

Liz had thought along the same lines herself. "At one point she complained about stomach issues. Maybe she contracted dysentery. We know conditions were unsanitary during the war."

"True." Julie frowned. "But that would negate our suspicions."

Which Liz figured Julie was not hoping for. The more spectacular the story, the bigger the splash for her article. People loved a good scandal, even a historical one. Emma's story was proving to be as outrageous as they came.

"Maybe there wasn't anything nefarious going on," Liz said. "Perhaps it was just a bitter man upset over having lost his true love."

"Yes, but Frederick's first visit was a year after the war, his second six months later," Julie countered. "If Emma had contracted the disease during her time spent disguised as a soldier, wouldn't she have gotten sick sooner?"

Liz blew out a breath. "That's a good point."

"We have to go back to the Ashby theory."

"That John intentionally made Emma sick? What did he have to gain? He already had access to her inheritance." Liz shook her head. "It seems extreme."

"And this entire situation isn't? From the bones and the contents of the plastic bag, to finding out about Emma and Frederick?"

Julie had a point.

"Why else would Althea want this covered up?" Julie insisted. "It must be true."

"We don't know that Althea wants it covered up. Not for sure. And Emma might just have gotten sick. End of story."

By the mutinous pout on Julie's lips, Liz could tell the other woman didn't agree. At this point, Julie was out to pin anything she could on the Ashby connection, thereby bringing Althea down as she catapulted herself into the newly vacated limelight.

"I could always drive down to Georgia," Julie suggested.

"That's above and beyond," Liz told her. "Besides, Emma never made it to Macon, so I don't think you'd find anything pertinent."

She shrugged. "All I want is to get to the truth."

And publish it in a groundbreaking paper. Yes, Liz knew. "I'm getting fresh coffee. Want another cup?"

Julie, intently focused on something she was reading, simply nodded her head.

As Liz went to the kitchen, the inn phone rang. She detoured to the foyer. "Olde Mansion Inn. How may I help you?"

"Liz? This is Clara Parks."

"Hello, Clara. How are—"

"Someone's been in my house."

"Excuse me?"

"I noticed some of my things were disturbed, and a box of records is missing."

A swift chill ran over Liz's body. "Are you sure? You have been getting ready to move."

"I'm sure." Clara hesitated, but Liz didn't miss the nervousness in her voice. "I wasn't completely up front about the information I had on Emma. I gave you the journal, but there was more. And now it's gone."

The chill now morphed to full-fledged concern. "Have you called the police?"

"Yes. They're sending an officer by, but what can I tell him? A box is missing? An old lady lost a bunch of paper and such? I won't reveal the contents, so how much help can he be?"

"Why don't I come by?" Liz offered. "If you won't tell the police, maybe you can confide in me."

Clara, clearly distracted by the crisis, agreed. "Yes. You can—"

Liz heard a doorbell in the background.

"That must be the officer," Clara said.

"I'll be there soon," Liz promised before signing off. She hurried to her quarters to get her purse and then walked straight to the sitting room. "I need to go."

Julie looked up. "Go? Where?"

"Clara Parks's house. Someone broke in."

"What? Is she okay?"

"Shook up, as you'd imagine." Liz gathered the journal, her notes, and the other materials Julie had brought to the inn and carried them back to her room. She quickly locked them in the deep bottom drawer of her desk, her main concern getting to Clara.

"I'm coming with you." Julie grabbed her purse and followed Liz to the door. "Did she call the police?"

"Yes."

"Then why call you? Are you two close?"

"Not really." Liz dug her car keys from her purse. "But this involves Emma."

They jumped into Liz's car, and she concentrated on following the route Jackson had taken a few days earlier. Usually Liz found the Amish buggies quaint, but as she tried and failed to pass a slowly moving horse-drawn wagon, she barely kept her patience in check. By the time they reached Clara's house, a Pleasant Creek patrol car was backing out of the driveway. Liz waited until he pulled onto the main road before coming to a halt near the house.

Clara waited on the porch, her face drawn, her hands locked in a white-knuckled clench.

"We're here." Liz swiftly hurried up the sidewalk. "This is Julie. She's a historian working on Emma's story."

Julie nodded in a solemn greeting.

"I'm so glad you came," Clara said, leading them inside. "The officer made a report, but he couldn't do much."

"Tell me what happened."

Clara led them to the dining room. "I first noticed some of the boxes I'd dragged down from the attic were moved. When I examined them, I found one missing. Thinking I'd placed it elsewhere, I scoured the entire downstairs. When I went back, I realized the missing box had records and documents and keepsakes from when the Parkses worked at the Ashby residence."

Julie perked up. "Are there more?"

Liz groaned inwardly.

"Some pictures, maybe," Clara said. "But the important keepsakes were in that box."

"And you're sure someone took it?"

"After I determined the box was gone, I got a bad feeling. So I looked again and found paperwork disturbed on a desk in the spare bedroom. The drawers had been rifled through as well."

Nerves danced in Liz's belly again. "This is serious, Clara."

Clara nodded, shaky. "I called my niece. She's offered to let me stay with her until I move."

Liz glanced at the boxes. "Who knew you had this information?"

"My family, of course. I told you the Parkses kept secrets, but obviously someone else knows. Beyond you, I don't know."

"Althea?" Julie asked.

"Probably. She's called many times looking for any Ashby history I might have, but I always turned her down." Clara barked an uneasy laugh. "Her assistant called too, thinking I might give her the information I had refused Althea."

"Do you honestly think Althea would sink this low to find out about Emma and her family?" Liz asked.

Clara held up her hands. "I really can't say. Somebody did."

Julie pulled her cell from her purse. "Let me give Lesley a call. She would know what Althea's been doing."

Clara nodded in approval as Julie left the room. Liz walked over to the stack of boxes. "I have to admit, the timing seems more than coincidental. You only gave me the box with Emma's journal a few days ago."

Rubbing her hands over her arms, Clara asked, "Besides Jackson, who knows you have it?"

"The Material Girls and Julie."

"This is very upsetting."

Liz took Clara's arm and led her to the living room, helping the older woman take a seat on the couch. Her coloring was still too pale for Liz's liking. She hated the idea of Clara being all alone and scared.

She wanted to call Jackson. He was so calm and steady. Having his presence there might help. Liz fished in her purse but came up empty. Then she remembered rushing from the inn and leaving her cell on the table.

Okay. She'd deal with the situation on her own.

"I have to ask you something," Liz said as she took a seat beside Clara. "Did you leave the photo and letter on my property?"

Clara's eyes misted over.

"You can be honest with me," Liz urged gently.

"Yes. I'm sorry I pulled you into this."

"But why?"

"I'd forgotten about all the old boxes and memories until I started getting ready to move. When I came across Emma's journal, I recalled my parents' vow of secrecy, but also their insistence that there was more going on with Emma." Clara bit her lower lip before continuing. "Emma's death was over a hundred years ago. All I had to go on were stories handed down in my family, always vague and whispered. Then when I read her journal, I felt deep inside that there was more to the story. But I'm not a historian, so I didn't know what to do. And who would believe that an Ashby ancestor might have secrets to keep? They're an upstanding family."

Althea would have surely tried to stop any revelations that would bring bad publicity to her family name. Liz understood how Clara felt—unsure where to turn but harboring a deep desire to uncover the truth.

"I got the idea to leave an information trail one day when I was at Sew Welcome. Sadie wanted to get a cup of tea, so I went with her to the inn kitchen. While she made her drink, I looked out the back window. The lovely lilacs caught my eye. When I asked about them, Sadie told me that was your favorite place to relax. I still hadn't decided how to handle the journal. But after you solved the Peabody murder, I just knew you could help Emma."

"That's quite a stretch."

"Sadie and Mary Ann think very highly of you, and they told me you used to be a lawyer."

Humbled, Liz took Clara's hand. "You wanted me to find the letter and the photo."

"I should have told you. But when the bones were found, I got scared." Clara's eyes were still wet. "I had no idea there were any bones buried on the property."

"You certainly weren't the only one."

"Every time I went to Sew Welcome I asked about your progress, and Sadie filled me in. I decided to let you keep looking into Emma's history and left you the note in your kitchen." She squeezed Liz's hand. "I'm so sorry I wasn't truthful."

"I see why you didn't tell me. But I'm glad to finally learn it was you all along. Wondering who left the keepsakes and that note was keeping me up at night." Liz paused a moment and then looked at Clara. "I've been curious. Why wasn't the letter Emma wrote to Frederick in his possession?"

"According to family lore, Emma wrote it with every intention of sending it, but then she died. The letter never left the Ashby house."

"But one of your ancestors knew about it."

"Yes, someone in my family had been mailing the letters for Emma. But once she died, they decided to keep it instead. Perhaps that was the start of the vow. The letter packed an emotional punch. Coupled with the photo, I figured you wouldn't be able to resist looking into it."

"And since they were found on my property, I felt responsible."

"You figured me out," Clara said. "Now what do you make of this burglary?"

As the two women pondered that thought, Julie came back into the living room, her brow creased. "I can't get ahold of Lesley. She's not answering her cell or Althea Mitchell's house phone."

"Does she usually answer her calls or let them go to voice mail?"

"She answers—when I call, anyway." Julie glanced at her phone again. "She must be in the middle of something. I'll call back later." She looked at Liz. "What's going on in here?"

Liz didn't like the curious gleam in Julie's eyes. She turned to Clara, slightly shaking her head. She hoped Clara understood the signal to follow her lead. "I was comforting Clara after her scare."

"It's been an awful fright," Clara said, clearly picking up Liz's hint.

"Would you like us to stay a bit longer?" Julie asked. "Look for more boxes in your attic?"

Smooth, Liz thought.

"No. I'm going to pack an overnight bag and head to my niece's house." Clara gave Liz a hug. "Thank you for rushing over."

"We'll wait," Liz told her.

Clara went off to pack, leaving Liz alone with Julie. "I'm dying to know what was in that missing box."

"As was someone else," Liz said, "so much so that they snuck in and took it."

Julie shuddered. "Creepy."

"I'll feel better knowing Clara is safe elsewhere."

"Where does that leave us?"

"I think we still need to focus on Emma. She's the key."

Five minutes later, Clara walked into the room with a small suitcase and purse. "I'm ready now."

Liz helped her lock up then followed Clara to her niece's house in town. As Clara got out of her car and waved, Liz headed back to the inn.

Once there, Julie declined Liz's invitation to come inside for something to eat. "It's late. I should be heading home."

"Thanks for everything, Julie."

Despite the younger woman's penchant for thinking only about her paper and the celebrity it might bring her in academic circles, Liz appreciated her hanging in there as things turned riskier.

After Julie left, Liz went straight to Sew Welcome. She needed her friends' support and wisdom right now. Just before she entered the shop, she heard voices, high-pitched with worry. As she entered, she spotted Sadie and Mary Ann by the counter, comforting Opal, who was dabbing her eyes with a tissue.

Mary Ann crossed the room, her expression troubled. "Liz. Thank goodness you're here. I tried to call you."

"I left my cell on the sitting room table." She nodded to Opal. "What's happened?"

"Althea's been taken to the hospital."

17

In a flash, the possible reasons Althea could be in the hospital crossed Liz's mind. "What on earth happened, Opal?"

"I'm not sure. I called in the morning, and Althea complained that she felt horrible. I was worried, so I checked in with her later. Lesley answered the phone and said she was taking Althea to the emergency room."

That explained why Julie couldn't get ahold of her friend. Lesley had been with Althea.

"Should we go to the hospital?"

Opal's expression brightened a small degree. "We could sit with Lesley. I know Althea's husband is out of town."

Sadie reached behind the counter to collect her purse. "I'm coming with you." She glanced at Mary Ann. "If you don't mind."

"Of course not. I'll hold down the store. Keep me informed."

Liz grabbed her phone before they left, and the three women hurried out to Liz's car. On the ride to the hospital, Sadie comforted Opal in her no-nonsense way. "No sense in worrying. She might already be right as rain for all we know."

Liz couldn't help but consider that all the stress over Emma and the revelation of family secrets had caused Althea to become sick. Guilt weighed heavily on her.

They rushed into the emergency waiting room to find Lesley on the phone, carrying on a heated conversation by the look of it. She spoke harshly into the cell, her expression abruptly calming when she saw the visitors. Ending the call, she dumped the phone in her bag and stood.

"I'm glad you came."

"We're so worried," Opal said.

"Any news?" Sadie asked, getting right to the point.

"Nothing official, but I think I know what might have happened."

Opal sank into one of the plastic chairs. "Tell us."

"Althea has been stubborn about her medication. Even though she hasn't felt well, she insists on measuring out her own doses. I think she might have overmedicated or gotten the medicines mixed up."

At the news, Liz and Sadie also sat.

"Her heart was racing," Lesley continued, "and she had a serious headache. She refused to leave the house. I had to force her."

"Thank goodness you did." Opal closed her eyes for a long moment. Liz said a silent prayer.

When Opal opened her eyes again, she turned to Lesley. "Does her husband know?"

"Yes. I called him just before we left the house. He's on his way home."

"I don't understand why Althea would let herself get so run down. It's not like her."

Lesley shot a quick glance at Liz before answering Opal. "It's the research she's been doing. Together, we've been uncovering her family history, and she hasn't liked what we've come across."

"All because of Emma," Liz said.

Lesley nodded. "Ever since you discovered the photograph and the letter, Althea's world has been tipped upside down. Her reputation is very important to her, and this revelation about her ancestors has upset her greatly."

Sadie patted Lesley's shoulder. "Is there anything we can do?"

"I wouldn't mind if you sat here with me until the doctor comes out."

The group settled back to wait. Liz called Mary Ann, sure her friend was anxiously awaiting news. Liz filled her in and assured her they'd keep her in the loop.

Doctors came in and out of swishing doors, speaking with worried relatives in hushed tones as they discussed the prognoses for their loved ones. Antiseptic and the air of despair made Liz uneasy until a whimsical thought hit her. If only she could bring the magical scent of Naomi's bakery here to encourage those waiting. Sweets always had a way of brightening up any situation, and this place needed some cheer.

Lesley's cell phone rang. She looked at the screen but didn't answer. Liz didn't blame her. She wouldn't want to answer questions right now.

After twenty minutes, Sadie rose from her chair. "Anyone want coffee? Something to eat?"

Liz declined, as did the others. Her stomach was in a knot, and the idea of drinking hospital coffee held little appeal.

Sadie took off. Lesley's phone rang again. Her expression was one of annoyance as she looked at the screen. "Excuse me," she said, answering the phone and moving to the far corner of the room. After a few terse words, she returned.

"Problem?" Liz asked.

"Nothing I can't handle," Lesley answered.

Tired of sitting, Liz got up to pace. She'd made four circuits back and forth when her own cell phone rang. Caller ID showed Caitlyn's number.

"What's going on?" Caitlyn demanded as soon as Liz said hello.

"Bad news travels fast."

"I work at the hospital, remember? And this *is* Pleasant Creek."

Liz reported what she knew, which wasn't much.

"It makes sense," Caitlyn said. "If Althea mixed up her meds, she could get very sick in a hurry."

"We're hoping that's all it is."

"Keep me posted."

Liz said goodbye as Sadie power-walked into the room.

"I have news," she informed them.

"How?" Lesley asked. "The doctor hasn't even come out yet."

Sadie grinned. "I have my ways."

"Spill it," Liz urged.

"You were right, Lesley. Althea mixed up her meds and had a bad reaction."

Opal placed a hand over her chest. "Is she going to be okay?"

"I would think so. Once they get her straightened out."

Liz's relief turned to confusion. "Wait. How did you find this out?"

Sadie winked. "I know people. They tell me things."

Liz didn't want to know. Plausible deniability.

As they spoke, a nurse approached them. "Are you Mrs. Mitchell's family?"

"No," Lesley answered for the group. "But I brought her in."

"No immediate family is here?"

"Her husband is on the way. Will she be all right?"

"I'm afraid I can't say." The nurse looked at them with regret. "Patient confidentiality. You understand."

Liz nodded. "Of course."

"But I can tell you that we are keeping her here tonight for observation. Check back tomorrow during visiting hours." The nurse smiled reassuringly and left.

Opal let out a long sigh. "I must say, I'm relieved. The nurse didn't act like Althea's condition was dire."

"What do you say we go back to the inn?" Liz suggested. "Lesley, would you like to join us? I can put something together for dinner."

Lesley hooked her purse strap over her shoulder. "Thanks, but I think I'll head back to the house to get things ready for when Mr. Mitchell comes home."

As they walked outside, the sun began to sink in the evening sky. The heat wave had passed, and although the air had cooled off, the asphalt was still warm from the sunny afternoon.

Opal stopped Lesley by placing a hand on her arm. "Thanks so much for looking after Althea."

"All part of the job. I'm glad I was there when she needed me."

Liz recalled snarky Julie's description of her friend's job. Lesley was a research assistant, not a nursemaid. Still, if it hadn't been for Lesley forcing Althea to get help, who knew what would have happened?

"I'll see you all tomorrow," the young woman said, pulling her cell phone from her purse as she walked to her car.

"C'mon." Liz motioned. "Let's get home."

She tossed her phone to Sadie who called Mary Ann on the drive, informing her that Althea would be spending the night at the hospital, and the ladies were going to have dinner at the inn. By the time they arrived, Mary Ann had closed the shop and was in the kitchen making sandwiches.

"I thought you might be hungry, so I started preparing without you."

Sadie bustled into the room, heading straight for the pantry. "I need a strong cup of tea."

"Thanks, Mary Ann," Liz said. "We aren't exactly sure that Althea is out of the woods, but the nurse seemed like she was trying to reassure us even though she wasn't allowed to tell us anything specific." Her stomach chose that moment to growl. "I don't know about you, but I am starving."

"I should get home," Opal said. "George will be worried."

"I put your tote in the sitting room."

"Thanks, Mary Ann. I'll talk to you ladies tomorrow."

After a round of comforting hugs, Opal left. Sandwiches made, the women sat on stools around the kitchen island, eating. Beans roamed the room, occasionally whining.

"Go lay down, boy."

When he whined again, Mary Ann shook her head. "I fed him just before you got home. He was acting strangely then too."

"Maybe he missed me."

Beans laid down at Liz's feet, his tail thumping.

"Or maybe I haven't been paying enough attention to him." After a vigorous tummy rub and a bit of ham sandwich, Beans dozed off.

Once she finished her own ham and cheese, Liz let out a long breath. "This is all my fault."

"I've been waiting for this," Sadie said, a scowl wrinkling her forehead. "And I'm here to tell you that just isn't so."

"If I hadn't been so set on uncovering Emma's past, Althea would be fine."

"You don't know that. And besides, she would have eventually found the truth on her own. She'd already begun looking into Emma."

"This whole thing started with Beans digging up the bones and plastic bag. You certainly didn't put them there," Mary Ann reasoned.

"True, but I finally found out who planted the bag."

Mary Ann's eyes widened. "Who?"

"The same person who left the note in the kitchen. Clara Parks." A stunned silence filled the room.

"I should have known," Sadie finally said. "Makes sense the way she'd been asking about the hunt every time she came into the shop. And with her family history entwined with the Ashbys, I should have put two and two together."

"You're slipping, my friend," Mary Ann teased.

"Which won't happen again." Sadie took a bite of her sandwich.

"But why would Clara do this?" Mary Ann asked.

"Because you both made her believe she could trust me." Liz told the women all that Clara had confided in her. "She figured if the contents of the plastic bag were found on my property, I'd get involved. She was right. The only thing she hadn't expected were the buried remains."

"And now Althea is ill," Mary Ann said. "I wonder if she really has any idea how convoluted Emma's story has become."

"I'm not about to ask her." Liz rose to carry her dish to the sink. "I think she's had enough of me."

"Do you think she deserves to see the journal?" Sadie asked.

Liz turned and leaned a hip against the counter. "At this point, I think all the cards should be placed on the table. I'll talk to Clara and see what she thinks. Between the break-in at her house and Althea in the hospital, the time for keeping secrets is over."

Mary Ann folded her napkin and tossed it on her empty plate. "I couldn't agree more."

"The journal has opened doors to the truth," Sadie said. "It might be useful to everyone now."

Liz frowned. "Earlier, Julie and I were discussing Emma's tone in the journal. It went from clear and concise to disorganized and confused. We know she was ill, but Julie can't get away from Frederick's theory that something bad happened to Emma. Would you mind looking over the journal and giving me your opinions?"

Both women nodded.

"It's in my room. I'll be right back."

Liz made her way to her quarters and flicked on the light switch. At her desk, she noticed the bottom drawer was ajar. But she was sure she'd locked it. Taking a tentative step closer, she noticed scratches in the wood around the lock. Pulling the drawer completely open, she gasped.

It was empty.

"This can't be," she whispered.

Turning on her heel, she rushed back to the kitchen. At her rushed approach, Beans stirred and barked.

"It's gone! The journal. My notebook. The research papers. All of it."

Mary Ann turned. The plate she'd been rinsing clattered into the sink.

"Gone?" Sadie echoed.

"I locked everything in my desk when Julie and I took off after Clara's call. Someone has stolen it all."

Mary Ann crossed the room and sank onto a stool. "First Clara's house, and now someone has broken in here?"

Liz joined the women at the island. "Mary Ann, did you notice anyone strange at the inn while we were at the hospital?"

"No. But a few customers came in. I have to admit, I was anxious to hear from you, so I stayed by the phone."

"And Sarah had already left for the day." Liz dragged her fingers through her hair.

"Maybe Julie came back?"

"Of course." Liz jumped up to fish her cell phone from her purse. Despite the late hour, she called. When Julie answered, Liz blurted out everything. Her stomach dipped at the ensuing silence. Julie couldn't believe the journal was gone.

Liz tossed the phone on the island. "Whoever did this must have been the same culprit who targeted Clara's house. Someone doesn't want the truth of Emma's story told. But who? And why?"

"I hate to say it," Sadie said in a quiet tone, "but Althea has the best reason to keep the truth from coming to light."

"After all she's been through, I hate to agree." Liz puffed out a frustrated breath. Beans bumped his nose against her leg. She crouched down to scratch his head. "But she's in the hospital. That's a pretty airtight alibi."

Mary Ann tapped her finger on her lower lip. "Julie cares, but why steal the journal? She has full access to it."

"She may want to outdo Althea, but I agree, why? She's right in the thick of our research." Liz glanced at the kitchen clock mounted on the wall. "It's getting late. Why don't you two head home."

"What about you?" Mary Ann asked as she and Sadie rose.

"I'm going to tear apart my room to see if anything else was taken, which I doubt. In the morning I'll call the police and hope I don't scare off any more of my guests."

18

Early the next morning, Chief Houghton came to the inn. Sarah took care of breakfast duty while Liz showed the chief of police the scene of the crime.

He took notes and said he'd file a report. "I'm not happy about the events taking place in my town."

"Trust me, I don't like the events taking place in my inn." Liz gestured to the damage done to her desk. "After I got over the shock of finding the research gone, I noticed all the drawers with locks were tampered with."

"Someone searched until they found what they were after. Is anything else missing?"

"No."

"I'll send an officer to dust for prints."

"Thanks. I appreciate you coming personally."

"I was going to stop by anyway. We got the results back on the bones. The lab reports that the remains are a female in her mid to late twenties."

A chill passed over Liz.

"And they're old. Your property was not the original burial place. They'd been moved."

"Moved?"

"Yes. There were multiple dirt samples found with the remains. The report states that the samples taken from your yard have a different composition than the other dirt found in the mix."

"Can the lab still check for DNA?"

"They'll try. Without a sample to compare it with, I don't know how successful they'll be."

"Now what?"

"I investigate your theft, and you lock your doors."

"Kind of hard to do with guests and customers coming and going."

"Try your best."

Liz bit the inside of her cheek. A lot of help he was.

"Let me know if you notice anyone suspicious hanging around."

"I will. Thanks."

Shortly after the chief left, Officer Dixon arrived to dust for fingerprints. By the time he departed, Liz's room was covered in a film of fine powder. She grabbed a cloth to clean up, not feeling any better about the entire investigation. The revelation about the bones had sent her thoughts into overdrive, trying to imagine who they belonged to. Logic told her that they shouldn't be Emma's. She was buried in the Ashby family plot. So whose remains were they?

By the time she finished cleaning up the powder, Liz had come up with an idea. She'd spent the bulk of her time focusing on Emma. It was time to take a look at the Ashby family's activities during the time period of Emma's journal.

She called Julie, told her about the change in direction, and asked her to get on it. Julie eagerly agreed.

As much as Liz wanted to do all of the research herself, she had duties at the inn that took priority, and she knew she needed help. Cleaning always cleared her mind, so she was hopeful her tasks would help her process what she already knew.

Mary Ann checked in when she arrived to open Sew Welcome. She found Liz in the kitchen, putting away cleaning supplies. "Did you sleep well last night?"

"No," Liz said. "I tossed and turned until it was time to get up and start breakfast."

"Me too. I thought about coming in early, but instead, I worked in the garden for a while. It's amazing how busywork can give you peace."

Liz nodded. "I spoke to the chief and reported the break-in, but he had news of his own. The remains found in the backyard belong to a woman in her twenties."

"Emma?"

"According to Althea, she's buried in the family plot. Unless the lab gets something useful back from DNA testing, if that's even possible, we won't know."

"But with the timing of everything that's happened . . ."

"It can't be her . . . can it?"

"Did the chief warn you off the case?"

"No. He's too concerned with finding the burglar. But I'd keep going even if he had."

Mary Ann smiled. "I didn't expect you to stop. Not now."

Liz closed the cabinet door. "My guests are gone, and I don't have anyone checking in until Thursday. The Hastings are coming back, and, oh, I nearly forgot." She smacked her hand on her forehead as she remembered why Mrs. Hastings was so keen to return this weekend. "The awards banquet is Saturday night. I hope Althea can make it, seeing as she's being honored."

"Opal spoke to her husband. It was a prescription mix-up. Once they regulate her meds, she should be back to normal. Maybe receiving an award will perk her up and put her in a better frame of mind."

"Until then, I have a little free time. This afternoon, I'm going to pay a visit to Bert Worth. I think he can help on a new avenue of information."

After changing out of her work clothes, Liz pulled on a sleeveless blue blouse and khaki capri pants, slipping on the sparkly sandals she loved. Her makeup was light enough to survive the warm temperature, and even though she brushed her hair into a smooth sheen, once she hit the humidity all bets were off.

She drove to the courthouse, parked, and walked into the building just in time to see Jackson coming down the stairs from his office.

"Liz, I heard what happened. I was headed out to the inn to see if you were okay."

Liz smiled, touched by his obvious concern. "I'm fine, aside from being upset over losing Emma's journal and my research notes."

"Do you have any idea who did it?"

"Unfortunately, no. The police are looking for suspects."

Jackson frowned. "I don't like this."

"That makes two of us."

"I can imagine how upsetting this must be," he said. "So what brings you here?"

"I need to talk to Bert. Do you know if he's in his office?"

"He is. I bumped into him earlier."

"Great. Thanks, Jackson. It was good to see you," Liz said, anxious to get to Bert before he ducked out for the day.

"Are we still on for the awards banquet?"

Liz met his gaze. "Wouldn't miss it."

Jackson smiled. "I'll pick you up at six."

"I'll be ready," Liz called over her shoulder as she speed-walked to Bert's office. She was a woman on a mission. The door was open, so she rapped on the doorframe and took a step inside. "Hello? Anyone home?"

Bert looked up from a large book he was holding. "Liz. Welcome."

"Sorry to barge in unannounced. Are you free?"

"Always, for you." Bert gestured to a chair.

Liz thanked him as she sat. "I have some questions that I'm hoping you can help me with."

"Shoot."

"I want to find out more about the Ashby family. Emma's husband, John, in particular."

Bert smiled knowingly. "I was thinking along those lines too."

"Since you probably know where to look, can you tell me what John did after returning from the war? And about any businesses or property he might have owned?"

"It would all be part of public records. What years in particular?"

Liz furrowed her brow. "Well, the war ended in 1865. I imagine it would have taken a while to get home and back into civilian life. How about 1866 up until he died?"

Bert took a pen and wrote the date on a blank pad of paper. "The records are downstairs. Care to join me?"

"I'd love to."

Bert led the way down to the record storage department while Liz caught him up on some of the more recent developments. He walked directly to a section where two microfiche machines were placed side by side on a desk. "Most of the old records were converted to microfiche decades ago. Only newer and more-requested records are digital. So we'll have to go old school."

He set up the reader like a pro. "I'm setting you up to research business owners in Pleasant Creek. Do you have something to take notes with?"

She held up the new notebook and pen she'd removed from her purse.

"I'll leave you to it while I look up property records."

Liz settled in. It had been a while since she'd used microfilm. But once her eyes adjusted, she adeptly scrolled through the information.

She wasn't sure how much time passed as she and Bert worked in silence. She'd found references to businesses owned by John Ashby. He'd owned many—multiple shops in town, but the bulk were factories.

Liz remembered reading that during the Restoration era after the war, industry grew in America. If John Ashby had benefited from Hartsfeld money, that would explain his many factories. He owned an ironworks, from which Liz discovered he made farm machinery and agricultural tools. There must have been high demand because the factories remained in the family until the 1940s. He also owned a successful chemical plant which had been sold in the early 1900s.

What has any of this got to do with Emma?

Determined to find some kind of link, she kept looking.

"This is strange."

Liz glanced at her partner in research. "What have you found?"

"Property records. I never knew this, but the land the inn was built on was owned by the Ashby family at one time."

"Really?" She scooted her chair over to see his screen. "When?"

"The family owned the land when they first settled in the area, well before the Civil War. But this part is curious. John Ashby sold the land in 1870."

"A few years after Emma died."

"It looks that way."

"Did he sell any other land at the time?"

Bert scrolled through the records. "No. Nothing else until after the turn of the century."

"His businesses seemed to be prosperous."

"Then perhaps Pleasant Creek was growing, and he saw the wisdom of selling the land."

"If anything, he was a savvy businessman," Liz said.

Bert took off his glasses and rubbed his eyes. "Has this helped?"

"I don't know. I feel like something's here, but I haven't connected the dots yet."

"This is how people get hooked on history. You have to keep at it until you get answers. Of course, by the time you have answers, you've got new questions." Bert pointed to her machine. "Anything else?"

"One more thing. Could you check the burial records for Emma?"

His eyebrow rose.

"Althea said Emma was buried in the family plot, but with all the conjecture on who the remains belong to, it wouldn't hurt to be sure."

"Give me a minute." He pulled out another set of records and scrolled through. "Here it is. Yes, Emma Ashby was laid to rest in the Ashby family plot."

Liz blew out a breath. "At least we know for certain."

While he closed down the machines, Liz collected her belongings.

She had a list, but didn't know where to go with it. "Bert, is there any way to check medical records from that time?"

"Possibly. It depends on what you want."

"We know Emma died of some kind of illness. If I could find out what it was, it might put one of my theories to rest."

"Let me look into it. I have a few places I can check."

"Are you sure you don't mind taking time away from your project?" Liz asked.

"Not at all. I'd like to help you get closure with Emma."

She hugged Bert. "You're the best."

The older man's face turned red beneath his fluffy gray hair. "Well, then . . . I'll call you if I find anything."

Liz waved goodbye and headed home. She envisioned a calm night snuggled into a cozy armchair in the library, reading a good book instead of research for a change. Still, there was a nagging sensation in the corner of her mind. After dinner, maybe a good fiction novel would relax her enough for the train of thought to come to light.

Sadie met her as she walked through the front door. "Good news. Opal talked to Althea. She's home resting."

Liz closed the door behind her. She almost locked it, but held off. Sew Welcome was still open for business. "I'm so glad. How is she?"

"Opal said Althea is back on her high horse, insisting she knows better than to keep all her meds in one place and has no idea how this could have happened. The doctors got her straightened out and warned her to take better care. Opal suggested she get one of those pill boxes with a compartment for each day, but Althea didn't like the suggestion."

"Maybe she's just being ornery after the scare of having to go to the hospital."

"Opal says Althea is insistent that she didn't mix up any pills."

Liz shook her head. "Why is she being so stubborn?"

"She doesn't like that she's getting forgetful." Sadie adjusted the big purple hat she wore, so the flowers weren't dangling in her face. "Comes with age, my dear."

Liz grinned. "I bet you don't forget a thing."

"Of course not. But I'm an exception."

They both laughed.

Sadie's grin slowly faded, and her expression turned serious once more. "There's more."

"There's always more," Liz said with a sigh.

"Althea hinted to Opal that she believes the medicine mix-up was foul play."

Liz blinked. "Why would she think that?"

"She heard about the burglaries and insists someone is out to get her."

"Is paranoia a symptom of mixed-up medications?"

Sadie shrugged. "I don't know, but she's convinced."

"Let's hope that once she's rested, her theory will go away. That is a very unsettling thought."

Mary Ann's voice floated down the hall. "Sadie?"

"Gotta run," Sadie said. "Miriam's holding a special preview class, and it's starting soon. Who knew having a talented quilter teaching the Amish style would be so popular?"

"You?"

"That's right," Sadie grinned with satisfaction. "Miriam's got a full class." With that good bit of news and a backward wave, she was off.

After Liz had eaten a light dinner, she was too restless to read. She went out back for a walk with Beans by her side.

"And to think," she said to the dog, "all this commotion started when you decided to expend a little energy. What would possibly possess you to do such a thing?"

Beans wagged his tail and trotted along happily until Liz took a seat at the bench surrounded by the lilac bushes. Kiera had done a fabulous job of getting her sanctuary back to normal.

"No digging," she told Beans. He looked up at her with what appeared to Liz to be a wide smile and then settled by her feet with a contented sigh. Apparently the walk from the house to the bench had satisfied his exercise quota for the day.

The lovely evening settled around Liz as the orange sun slowly descended in the darkening sky. The sweet fragrant flowers and the warm earth scented the night. Insects buzzed and in the distance, she heard a car horn honk. Taking a deep breath Liz closed her eyes, peaceful for the first time in two weeks. No wonder this was her favorite spot. After a few moments she began to doze.

The slam of a car door pulled her out of her catnap. Liz sat up and took in her surroundings. *Right. The bench. The lilacs. The plastic bag. The bones.*

She shivered. Would she always think about the remains when she came out here?

Glancing down at a snoring Beans, she smiled. At least one of them could sleep peacefully. Maybe tonight she'd actually get a few hours of shut-eye herself.

Althea came to mind. Would she sleep tonight or stay awake wondering if her medicine had been tampered with?

The more Liz thought about it, the more she also wondered. Had the organized and methodical Dr. Althea Mitchell been careless with her medication or had someone deliberately switched her pills?

19

On Wednesday morning, Liz slept in. Without any guests staying at the inn, she finally caught up on some much needed rest. When she got up, she felt ready to take on the world. She wondered if the world would cooperate.

Filled with energy, she went through the vacant rooms with a dust cloth to ready the place for the rest of the week. Mr. and Mrs. Hastings would be checking in on Thursday, and the remainder of the rooms would be filled through the weekend.

At noon, the inn phone rang as Liz was surfing the Internet, looking for breakfast inspiration.

"Olde Mansion Inn. How may I help you?"

"Liz, it's Bert Worth. I have something I think you'll want to see."

"Something to do with Emma?"

"Yes. Can you come to the courthouse?"

"You bet." They set a time, and Liz went to her quarters to get ready.

In her room, she texted Julie about Bert's phone call and assured the historian she'd get back to her later with any new leads. Minutes later, dressed in a cotton sundress and flats, Liz ran into Miriam as she hurried through the inn's foyer.

"Liz. I hoped to catch you before you got busy for the day."

"I'm headed out to an appointment, but I can spare a few minutes. What's up?"

From her tote bag, Miriam removed a medium-size four-patch block, quilted and bound around the edges. The colors were various shades of pinks, purples, blues, and greens. The fabric designs were floral, geometric, and solid. In opposite corners of the block were the stitched initials *E* and *F*. As Liz examined the piece closely, she also noticed dates stitched into the quilt top. In the floral piece, which resembled lilacs, was the current year. In a blue geometric piece was the year the Civil War ended.

"It's beautiful, but what does this mean?"

"You have been so captivated by the story of a woman you have never met. It is sad and romantic all at once. I had some leftover fabric and was at odds about what to do with it. Then it struck me. Would Liz want her own keepsake? You have put so much time and energy in discovering what you can about Emma, I thought perhaps you would like the memory of her to become a part of the inn." Miriam paused for a moment, her expression unsure. "Was I wrong to make this for you?"

Liz blinked back unexpected tears. "No. This is lovely. I'll treasure it."

Miriam beamed. "My girls helped. I let Grace piece the top on the family sewing machine. Keturah picked out the fabric from my leftovers, and she helped bind the block to finish it."

"I'm so impressed. Tell your daughters they did a beautiful job."

"They will be pleased to hear your kind words."

"The next time you bring them by the shop, may I have them join me in a tea party?"

"Most certainly. They will be excited."

Liz ran her fingers over the intricate quilting on the block. "Miriam, this is so sweet. Thank you."

Miriam ducked her head, but Liz could see the pleasure in her expression.

After they parted ways, Liz took the gift to her quarters, gently laying it at the end of her dresser. She'd figure out where to display it later. Right now, Bert was waiting.

She made it to the courthouse in no time. "I'm here!" she called out as she entered Bert's office.

Bert smiled, his eyes sparkling. His hair looked especially fluffy today, making Liz think of cotton candy.

"Come in. I have something to show you."

Liz hurried to the desk where Bert had spread out some papers.

"After you asked me to check into medical records, I had to think where to look. The current hospital hadn't been built yet during Emma's time. She most likely would have seen the local doctor. I went back to the town rolls and came across the name of the doctor practicing in Pleasant Creek at the time. Sorry to say, I wasn't able to locate any of his records, but as luck would have it, the doctor was later published in the *Journal of the American Medical Association*. I looked up his articles, and one in particular stood out to me."

"Let's hear it."

"The article was first published in 1884, about fifteen years after Emma died. In the article he referenced a young woman he'd treated. I believe it might have been Emma."

"Because . . . ?"

"His article was on arsenic poisoning. His case referenced a twenty-three-year-old woman who was besieged with headaches and gastrointestinal problems. There was no medical reason for her to have these symptoms, but she got progressively worse. Soon her hands and feet were numb. And near her death, her fingernails were cracked and discolored; a symptom he finally realized came from arsenic ingestion. In the article he lamented the fact that he hadn't understood the significance of these symptoms sooner. It wasn't until years later that he came across the correct diagnosis when he treated the same problem with another patient."

"So how does this tie to Emma?"

"You said she was ill. Do you know her symptoms?"

"Yes. She mentioned bouts of stomach problems, so we thought she might have contracted dysentery. She didn't write about the numbness until later." Liz blinked. "That would explain why her writing was so sloppy near the end of the journal."

Bert nodded.

"Okay, but without medical records, how can you be sure this is her?"

"Because after you left, I went back and looked at the businesses

John Ashby owned. His chemical factory produced arsenic which was the main ingredient in embalming fluid after the Civil War."

"Are you suggesting that John poisoned Emma?"

"I am."

Liz dropped into the nearby chair. "Wow. According to our research, Frederick, Emma's true love, said all along that there was foul play, but I dismissed it. Turns out he could have been right." The gravity of the news slowly began to sink in. "So John used arsenic . . ."

"An element with a historically nasty reputation as a poison."

Liz closed her eyes. "How horrible."

"Yes. I imagine it wasn't a pleasant way to go."

She looked up at Bert, hovering by her side. "What do I do with this information?"

"I'm certain you'll decide on the right course of action."

Bert handed her copies of the article and the research he'd done. Liz stuffed the papers into her purse and thanked Bert. Once outside, Liz felt untethered. She walked down Main Street, the noonday heat warming her shoulders. She thought about getting a latte, but her stomach protested. After a few indecisive minutes, she sat on a bench in the shade and made a call to the fabric shop.

"It's a beautiful day. Thanks for calling Sew Welcome," a cheerful voice answered.

"Mary Ann, are you busy?"

"Liz?"

"Yes. I need some advice." Liz explained Bert's findings and ended with the question that had been nagging at her since she'd discovered this disturbing information. "Do I tell Althea?"

"I think you already know the answer."

Mary Ann was right, of course. Liz just needed confirmation.

"This is going to truly upset her."

"Yes, but if you were able to find this information, so will the person who stole your research. Best if Althea hears it from you."

Liz puffed out a breath. "Oh, yay. Like she doesn't already hate me."

Her friend chuckled. "Give Althea a call. What's the worst that can happen?"

"Well, she'll either hang up on me or ask me to come over."

"I guess you'll find out."

After ending the call, Liz stared at her cell phone. She hated to be the bearer of bad news, but she supposed Mary Ann was right. Also, she reasoned that Althea would rather hear the theory from Liz now than read about it in an article by an ambitious academic rival.

Straightening her shoulders, Liz pulled up Althea's number and pressed the SEND button.

The phone rang a few times until a terse voice answered, "Dr. Althea Mitchell at your service."

Clearing her throat, Liz said, "Dr. Mitchell, this is Liz Eckardt. Are you free this afternoon?"

Althea's tone frosted. "Why? So you can come by and cast aspersions on my family again?"

That's exactly why. "I would like to talk to you."

Silence filled the space until Althea answered, "Fine. You may come by now."

The drive to Althea's house felt like it took forever. As she parked, Liz had to fight the urge to turn around, but in the end, her sense of right over wrong won out.

The door swung open as she stepped onto the porch.

"Let's keep this visit quick," Althea said in her imperial tone. "I have to work on my speech for the banquet."

Where was the ever-present Lesley, Liz wondered. She followed Althea to the living room where the rotund woman took her seat. Had her chair always resembled a throne?

"Well?" Althea snapped.

Liz sat on the couch, an uneasy sensation turning in her stomach. "How are you feeling?"

A bit of the haughtiness faded when Althea heard Liz's genuine concern. "Much better, thank you. I've rested and feel as good as new."

Right. Okay. *Stop procrastinating.*

Liz cleared her throat. "I honestly don't know where to start, so I'm going to go back to the beginning."

Recapping the discovery of the bones, her visits to this living room, revealing the discovery of the journal and its hidden photo, the burglaries, and her search into Ashby family history, Liz laid it all on the line. By the time she had finished, Althea was pale, but still in one piece.

"That is quite a story," Althea said after minutes of taut silence.

Opening her purse, Liz took out the papers Bert had given her and laid them on the coffee table. "Please know I never wanted to cause you grief. I simply needed to find out about the bones and the contents of the plastic bag that I found in my yard. I never imagined the truth would lead me here."

Althea's eyes skimmed over the papers before narrowing. "I should have known Clara Parks had a part in all this. The woman never gave me the time of day when it came to her secrets."

"She mentioned something about a vow."

Waving her hand in a lofty gesture, Althea scoffed. "Goodness, you'd think she was involved in a super-secret society for heaven's sake."

Liz couldn't hide her smile. Althea was taking this better than she'd expected. But still, the woman hadn't reacted to the accusation of murder.

"I suspected Clara had a journal, or at least some type of written record about my family. I've tried to get my hands on it for a long time now, but Clara is cagey. She ran me around in circles and still never admitted she had the book."

Liz had to ask. "Did you send someone to her house to steal it?"

"Absolutely not!" Althea thundered in pure affront. "Do I *want* an unflattering family history? No. But would I want historical records destroyed simply to keep the past buried? Never. I am a historian. As much as I value my family legacy, preservation of the past comes first. Clara never understood that."

Observing the formidable expression on Althea's face, Liz believed her. "Did you suspect your ancestor of . . . foul play?"

At Liz's question, Althea's shoulders slumped. Her face seemed to have gained more wrinkles in the time Liz had joined her in the living room.

"I'm not naive, Liz. Rumors of murder have been whispered in my family for years. John's second wife was my great-great-great grandmother." Althea smoothed her skirt, her hands moving in a nervous fashion. "If she knew anything about her husband's actions, she went to the grave—at a ripe old age, I might add—keeping those suspicions It was the household staff that perpetuated the story." Althea took a breath and met Liz's gaze head-on. "I admit, from what you've told me, all indications point to the possibility that my forefather killed his first wife."

"I'm sorry."

"As much as the truth is terrible, I have to ask myself, who would care enough about my family history to steal it?"

"A rival?"

Althea let out a mirthless laugh. "I have many in the academic world, but these people are scholars, not thugs."

"I wish I had the answer for you. Perhaps the police will be more successful on that front."

Althea ran a shaky hand over her brow. "Thank you for coming to me with this information."

"Will it affect the awards banquet this weekend?"

Again, Althea's steely gaze pierced hers. "That depends on you."

"In what way?" Liz asked.

"Obviously someone is after the truth of Emma's life and death. In time, these assumptions will be made public. But for now, I'm asking you to not reveal what you've learned. It's completely selfish of me, but I would like to decide the day I release this information, not someone else."

Liz could appreciate Althea's request. After all the woman had been through, it was the least Liz could agree to. "I'm okay with that."

"Very well."

A strained silence settled over them. Liz clutched her purse and rose. "I should let you get back to your work."

Althea walked with Liz to the front door.

"Good luck at the banquet," Liz said. "I look forward to seeing you accept your award."

The older woman's brows rose. "You're attending?"

"Opal invited me."

A genuine smile lit Althea's eyes. "She is a good friend. Who else would sponsor an entire table?"

"She's very excited." Liz moved down the few steps to the walkway, the uneasy feeling she'd had when entering Althea's house returning. She hesitated, not sure what to say, and then blurted, "Please be careful. I know it sounds strange, but I don't want anything to happen to you."

"Is this your way of saying you think I'm in danger?"

"All I know is that I'm still troubled about everything that's been going on. The police haven't found any leads in the burglaries yet. Opal said you were adamant about not mixing up your medication, but isn't the timing strange?"

"Liz, I appreciate your concern."

"Promise me you'll be careful."

A hint of a smile curved Althea's lips. "I promise."

Althea waved her off, and as Liz climbed into her car, she hoped Althea took her warning to heart.

20

Thursday morning, Liz bustled around the Somewhere in Time Room, placing one of Mrs. Hastings's favorite scented candles on the dresser. She loved having repeat customers and had decided to leave special treats in their rooms whenever her guests returned. She wasn't entirely sure if Mr. Hastings was going to join his wife, but just in case, she left a bowl of his favorite toffee candy. Tomorrow morning, cinnamon bread would be on the breakfast menu.

Just before noon, Liz headed out to Soap and Such, the shop on Main Street that featured custom-made soaps and lotions. The last time Mrs. Hastings had stayed, she'd mentioned liking their products. Why not have a bar of handmade soap waiting by the tub?

Eager to run her errand and get back quickly, Liz hurried to the shop and made her purchase. Her phone rang as she was paying, so Liz let it go to voice mail. She checked it once she left the store to find a message waiting for her from Julie, probably wanting an update. Liz planned to call her back after the awards ceremony. She owed Althea that much.

As she headed up the walkway to the inn, Clara Parks walked out the front door. She stopped short when she saw Liz.

"Clara. How are you?" Liz asked. The woman appeared calm, despite the break-in at her home.

"Fine. My niece has been taking good care of me."

Liz smiled, glad to hear good news for a change.

"I hear you've had some excitement around here."

"The burglar decided to visit the inn. The police are still investigating."

Clara nodded. "Much the same in my case."

"I still don't understand why the thief wants all the information on Emma. It's not like it's a current case. Emma's been gone for over a century."

A flash of what Liz guessed might be guilt flashed through Clara's eyes. "Secrets tend to bring out the worst in people."

Liz regarded her new friend for a moment. "You do know that Frederick insisted Emma was intentionally made sick."

"Yes. I had heard that."

"And John Ashby owned a chemical company. He could have poisoned Emma." Liz noticed that Clara didn't look surprised. "But then you already knew about it."

"I'm afraid so."

"Yet you kept another secret?"

"It's the Parks's vow. It was one thing to give you the journal but another to give you rumors. Even after all these years it's hard to shake old habits."

Leaning against the porch railing, Liz gazed up at Clara who stood in the shade of the wide porch. "I know for a fact that arsenic was produced in John's chemical factory."

"Oh dear."

"Let's sit."

They moved to a grouping of wicker furniture. Clara settled into the love seat, Liz in the rocker. Once seated, Liz studied the older woman. "I think the time has come to give up the vow."

Clara let out a long sigh. "There aren't any immediate Parkses left to keep the secret, not that it even matters anymore. I won't burden my niece with ancient history. And Althea has no use for the truth."

"You don't know that."

With a shrug, Clara said, "Only if it suits her."

"A few weeks ago I would have agreed with you, but now, I'm not convinced. Althea does want to know the truth, even if it puts her family in a bad light. Her present reputation as a historian is more important to her than the failings of her family in the past."

"Perhaps."

Liz hid a smile. Apparently Clara could be stubborn too. "What really happened?"

Clara picked at a thread on her skirt before meeting Liz's gaze. "The Parks family came up with the vow as a way to make sure John Ashby paid for murdering Emma."

Now that the truth was finally out in the open, Liz shivered.

"By all accounts the man was cold-blooded," Clara said. "When he found out about Emma and Frederick, he methodically and purposely set out to kill her. And he succeeded."

"Did your relatives know what he was doing at the time?"

"Not until the very end. At Emma's deathbed, thinking he would soon be rid of her, John Ashby asked his dying wife if arsenic tasted good. He admitted what he had done. Emma, a savvy woman until the very end, closed her eyes and appeared unresponsive. John left, thinking his wife to be at death's door. He made the mistake of leaving too soon. My relative sat with her, so she wouldn't be alone as she slipped away. Emma was able to whisper the truth of John's actions and point her to her hidden journal."

Liz let the truth of it all sink in. "So John assumed he'd gotten away with murder."

"Yes."

The two women sat in silence for a long time. Cars passed by the inn. A dog barked in the distance. Children's voices carried in the wind. A bee bounced from one flower to another.

"John eventually remarried. My relatives kept a vigilant watch over his new wife, but she was a timid woman who loved John and never did a thing that would cause him to hurt her."

"Why didn't your ancestors go the authorities?" Liz asked.

"Frederick was right about one thing. John had money—Emma's money, ironically—and influence. No one would believe that a fine pillar of the community like John would carry out such a heinous act, and the accusation of servants known to favor his wife wouldn't sway anyone."

"So he got away with it?"

A slight smile tugged at Clara's lips. "I didn't say that."

Liz tilted her head. "More secrets?"

"Let's just say John paid. My ancestors made sure of it."

"Do I want to know?"

"That's up to you."

Liz considered it and then said, "Yes."

"When Emma used her dying breaths to name her murderer to my ancestor, my ancestor made her a promise. Through the years John lost his holdings, one by one—businesses, properties."

"I didn't get that far in the records Bert and I looked up."

"He should have been more diligent in checking out those he hired to keep his books and manage his businesses. Just because someone didn't have the last name of Parks didn't mean he wasn't related."

"Sneaky."

"But effective."

Liz rocked back in her chair. "Althea has no knowledge of this?"

"No."

"Then it can't be Althea who stole the papers from your house. Why would she, when she has no idea of the entire story?"

"She might have thought things in her family history were fishy, but the Parkses would look just as bad as the Ashbys had the complete truth come out. Do you see why I never gave her anything when she contacted me?"

"I understand why you left the photo and letter on my property; to get the ball rolling. But this entire state of affairs is between your family and the Ashbys. Why would someone steal the information from me?"

"I don't know."

As her shoulders slumped, Liz rubbed her throbbing temples. "You know Althea deserves the whole truth."

"She does," Clara agreed quietly.

"But not until after the awards banquet. She's been through enough. Afterward, we'll go to see her. Together."

Clara reached out and patted Liz's arm. "I appreciate the offer, but telling the truth is on me. I must face Althea alone."

"I'd love to be a fly on the wall for that conversation."

The front door opened, and two chatting women holding large bags from Sew Welcome exited the inn.

Clara gathered her purse. "I'm sorry I dragged you into this, Liz. I had no idea things would get so out of hand. But I was right about one thing—you are a good detective."

Liz smiled. "I haven't solved the whole case, but life has certainly been exciting lately."

When Clara left, Liz sat on the porch, pondering the mystery of who broke into the inn. Worse, whose remains had Beans found? Would she ever find out?

She had just risen when she heard someone calling her name. Liz glanced over at the sound, a smile curving her lips as Mrs. Hastings hurried toward her with her husband trailing behind.

"Liz, I know we're early, but Donald insisted we leave the house at the crack of dawn this morning."

Mr. Hastings hurried to catch up. "Edna was afraid she'd miss all the news if we got here after check-in time."

"Donald, really. We've been looking forward to returning."

Liz tightened her hold on the bag from Soap and Such, and moved it behind her back, not wanting to reveal her surprise for Mrs. Hastings. "I'm so happy to see you both. Mr. Hastings, I wasn't sure you were coming."

"Edna insisted. She said there was more drama in Pleasant Creek than on television."

"I merely pointed out that there was a real-life mystery going on at the Olde Mansion Inn. Who would want to miss that?"

Liz chuckled at the couple's lively back-and-forth. "C'mon in. Let's get your bags up to your room, and then we can catch up."

"Any chance we can get a snack?"

"Donald!" Mrs. Hastings admonished.

"Well, we missed lunch in an all-fired hurry to get here."

Mrs. Hasting regarded Liz confidentially. "He exaggerates."

"And *he* can hear you," said Mr. Hastings.

Liz laughed. "As luck would have it, I have a fresh loaf of cinnamon bread with your name on it in the kitchen."

"I am a lucky man." Mr. Hastings smiled.

Mrs. Hastings harrumphed, but Liz didn't miss the twinkle in her eyes.

When Liz showed them to their room, she made a discreet visit to the bath to place the soap in a special dish before leaving her guests alone. Not ten minutes passed before Mrs. Hastings hunted down Liz, finding her in the kitchen.

"I see you left Donald a bowl of candy. I swear the only reason he agreed to come back this weekend is because you indulge him. Between the candy and the bread, he is indeed a very happy man." Mrs. Hastings stopped beside her. "And *I* noticed the soap. Thank you, Liz."

Liz sliced the bread. "What can I say? I have a soft spot for both of you." She nodded over her shoulder. "Tea is on the dining room table."

"It's like you read my mind."

Liz joined her guest and proceeded to bring her up to speed on Emma's story. For the first time since Liz had met the woman, Mrs. Hastings didn't say a word, her eyes going wide as Liz related the history they'd discovered in recent days.

Liz finished and sipped her tea, waiting for a response.

"My goodness. You have been busy."

Liz chuckled. "To be honest, when you told me you wanted to book a room for this weekend, I didn't expect to have much news."

"Nor did I expect such a story."

"I worry about how all this will affect bookings for the inn.

Thankfully, I have repeat customers like you and your husband." Liz cupped her hands around her teacup. "I'll be glad when this saga comes to an end and I can get back to a normal life."

"Normal is overrated."

"Perhaps. But ever since the letter and the photograph were found on the property, I've felt obligated to put Emma to rest. The right way."

Mrs. Hastings patted Liz's hand. "And I have no doubt you will."

Her guest's confidence warmed Liz's heart. "Now then, I have things to do before the other weekend guests arrive, and you should probably check on your husband."

"He brought a new book along to read this weekend, so I suppose I should see if he settled into that comfy armchair by the window and devoured all the candies you left him."

Liz tried to feel guilty but couldn't.

As Mrs. Hastings headed upstairs, Liz carried the teacups to the sink to rinse and place in the dishwasher. She'd just closed the door when a solid rap sounded at the utility-room door.

"I'm not expecting anyone," she murmured to herself as she opened the door to find Chief Houghton holding an evidence bag. "Chief. What are you doing here?"

He held up the bag. "Returning your things."

Liz opened the door wider. "Please come in."

The chief lumbered into the kitchen and then handed the bag to Liz. "Everything you listed as stolen was returned."

"I don't understand."

"One of my men found a box outside the station this morning. Imagine his surprise when it turned out to be the belongings you reported missing from the inn."

"This is so odd." Liz wrinkled her brow. "Why would someone take my papers, only to return them?"

The chief shrugged. "I've been a police officer for a long time,

Liz. I've learned that sometimes there's not enough information to explain human behavior."

She thought back to her years of practicing law and silently agreed.

"We dusted for prints, but I doubt we'll come up with a match. I have a feeling whoever took your research just wanted access to the information. Keeping the papers was a by-product they could do without."

Liz opened the plastic bag and carefully removed the contents, laying them out on the kitchen island. To her relief, the original photo was still intact. She gently flipped through the journal. She'd have to go through it later, but from what she could see, the book hadn't been damaged. "It's all here."

The chief nodded. "Glad to bring good news for a change."

"Were Clara Parks's things returned, by any chance?"

"No."

"Hmm. Well, at least there's hope. Perhaps the thief has a conscience."

"This has been an odd case, Liz. I have no idea what to expect."

"No disagreements there." She set the journal back on the island. "Any results on the DNA testing?"

"Nothing. The lab doesn't have anything to compare the bones we took from the property with. And since this isn't a current case, it isn't a priority."

"What about the journal? Emma touched it."

One brow rose. "You want me to look into a possible connection just because the remains were of a young woman?"

"A lot of things about Emma don't add up," Liz said. "Is there any chance a lab could extract a sample from this journal?"

"It's a long shot, but we could try. Who knows what they might find."

Liz bit her lip. Did she dare part with the journal again? "Tell you what, after the awards banquet I'll get the journal to you for testing. I need to talk to a few people before I let you have it."

"Sounds good." The chief walked to the door. "Don't expect much. It's very probable any DNA has degraded with time."

"I understand."

"Okay, I'm off." Chief Houghton smiled at her. "I did my good deed for the day. Now it's back to running the station and catching bad guys."

"In the hotbed of crime that is Pleasant Creek."

"Your tax dollars at work." The chief tapped the brim of his hat and then strode back through the utility room and out the door.

Liz had followed the chief and closed the door behind him. When she stepped back into the kitchen, her gaze was drawn to the contents of the evidence bag on the island. She was especially happy to have the journal back in her possession. Overwhelming relief filled her as she locked them away. This time, she opted for the inn's safe instead of her desk drawer.

Still, so many questions remained. Who committed the burglaries? What was the real story about Althea's medicine? Who had been reburied on the inn's property? And *why*?

21

Just before six o'clock on Saturday night, Liz fastened her necklace, smoothed her black sheath dress, and slipped into black heels. She hadn't really dressed up since she'd moved from Boston. It felt good to fuss over her appearance. Grabbing her clutch and floral pashmina shawl, Liz set off for the foyer.

To her delight, she found Mrs. Hastings in a serious conversation with Jackson, who looked vaguely like he regretted arriving early. When Liz walked into the room, his expression brightened considerably.

"Liz, you didn't tell me you had such a handsome date for the banquet tonight." Mrs. Hastings winked.

"Jackson isn't my date. I'm his bodyguard," Liz said in her most official voice. "It's my job to keep the mayor safe."

Mrs. Hastings shook her head at Liz. "The mayor has promised to watch out for *you* tonight, what with all the excitement going on in Pleasant Creek. I still can't believe all I missed while I was at home."

"It has been a whirlwind," Liz said.

Her eyes twinkling, Mrs. Hastings asked, "Do you expect any excitement tonight?"

"None," Liz answered firmly.

"Well, that's no fun," Mrs. Hasting grumped.

Liz hoped that the night would be drama-free. She put the lingering questions about Althea's medication, Clara's burglary, and the DNA testing aside. These things wouldn't be resolved tonight.

"Sleep well and I'll talk to you tomorrow," Liz said, although she suspected Mrs. Hastings would be awake and waiting for a full report when she returned. She'd noticed that the coziest chair in the four-season room was set up for a long night with a thick mystery novel, a footstool, and an electric mug warmer.

"Don't let me keep you. You two go on now," Mrs. Hastings said as she bustled them out the door.

The day had cooled off, and rain clouds rolled in. It cloaked them in humidity and gloom, and the general chill of the atmosphere put Liz on edge. *This is supposed to be a fun night out.*

"Are all of your guests like her?" Jackson asked once he and Liz were off the porch.

"Mrs. Hastings is a bit of a mama bear. It's sweet." She chuckled. "There've been other quirky guests, but mostly quirky in a charming way."

"You must be building a good reputation."

"A reputation for mystery, a hearty breakfast, and open arms for amiable eccentrics? Definitely."

In the inn's small parking lot, Liz's brows rose when she glimpsed his shiny black sedan. "No truck?"

Jackson chuckled. "Tonight we travel in style."

Liz's eyes roamed from the dark sedan to Jackson. He'd dressed in a tailored black suit with a crisp white shirt and red tie. Very dapper—and exceedingly handsome. "I'm all for style."

The drive to the banquet hall didn't take long. Liz enjoyed the ride and Jackson's company. He was the kind of man a woman could easily lose her heart to—attractive, smart, a true gentleman. If she wasn't careful . . .

People streamed into the building as Jackson parked. He turned to her before killing the ignition. "Ready?"

She let out a breath. "Yes. Here's hoping Althea's night goes smoothly."

Liz and Jackson maneuvered through the room to find their assigned table. Mary Ann was already seated beside Sadie, who was sporting a stylish black pillbox hat complete with veil and feathers. They were both chatting with George.

Sadie glanced up. "You made it."

"I wouldn't dream of missing tonight," Liz said as she placed her clutch and shawl on an empty chair. "Where's Opal?"

Mary Ann pointed to a table near them. "Talking to Althea."

To Liz's great relief, Althea looked much better than the last time she'd seen her. Her cheeks had a healthy glow that was brought out by her eye-catching fuchsia dress with matching hair bow.

When Opal returned, she had a wide smile on her lips. "Isn't this exciting? The president of the genealogy guild is here to personally present Althea with the award."

"Looks like Althea is in her element tonight," Jackson said.

"Is the man seated at Althea's table her husband?"

Jackson glanced over and nodded. "Herbert Mitchell. He doesn't usually go for these events."

"Maybe he's here because of Althea's health scare."

Liz only recognized one other person at the head table, Althea's assistant, Lesley. The young woman was busy typing on her smartphone instead of interacting with the others seated at the table. A frown wrinkled Lesley's brow as she concentrated on her task.

People mingled, enjoying appetizers before the main event. Dinner would be served next, and then the awards ceremony would take place. Liz found herself nervous on Althea's behalf.

Minutes before the meal was served, Naomi and Caitlyn arrived.

"Sorry, I had to work an emergency and couldn't leave right way," Caitlyn explained.

"And I wasn't about to leave without her," Naomi chimed in.

"The Material Girls are all accounted for," Sadie announced with a satisfied nod.

Soon the waiter brought plates of roasted chicken and vegetables. As they ate, Liz scanned the room. At one point, she noticed Lesley craning her neck as she looked at the banquet hall entrance. *Searching for someone?* Althea held court, chatting away, clearly enjoying herself. The others at the table listened, interjecting occasionally.

When the dinner plates were cleared away, the waiters poured coffee and brought dessert, and the awards ceremony began. A distinguished-looking man in a dark suit stepped onto the dais. An overhead spotlight targeted his gray hair slicked back above patrician features smoothed in a cool mask. He thumped the microphone on the podium and then cleared his throat before speaking.

"Good evening. For those who don't know me, my name is Walter Kenyon. On behalf of the Indiana Genealogy Guild, I welcome you to our annual awards banquet."

Applause erupted around the room. After a few moments, Walter held up his hand. "As you know, each year the guild acknowledges a member who has gone above and beyond in the area of genealogy. Whether it is educating the general public about what we do or making a new historical discovery, we at the guild annually honor a member who has been instrumental in getting our name into the public eye and advancing the field.

"This year, the member we have chosen to receive this award has done much to bring history to the public. With contributions as varied as her work with the local school system to nationally published historical papers, this recipient has worked tirelessly to help others uncover the past." He paused, smiled at the crowd, and said, "Please, join me in congratulating this year's Master of Genealogy Award winner, Dr. Althea Mitchell."

Applause broke out again. Althea rose, bowed to the room, and then joined Walter on the dais. They spoke a few words before he handed her a plaque; then he stepped back while she took over the podium.

"Thank you. Thank you, my friends." Althea beamed, holding her plaque close to her chest. "I am so humbled to receive this award. Most of you know how I have looked forward to this day. History is my life, and I can't think of a better way to share my passion than to help others enjoy delving into the past. Why, if not for the past, what would we have to build upon? It's like I always say—"

Before she had a chance to finish, a voice rang out from the back of the room. "Even if the past is a lie?"

Murmurs buzzed through the crowd. Liz turned toward the familiar voice, her eyes wide as she watched Julie make her way to the dais.

"Did you know she was going to be here?" Opal asked Liz, her voice shaky.

As astonished as everyone else in the room, Liz didn't know what to say. She shook her head no. *What is Julie up to?*

By this time, confusion marred Althea's joyful expression. "Excuse me?"

Julie climbed the steps to the platform. "Mr. Kenyon, you should know that Althea Mitchell is a fraud."

"Oh dear me," Liz said as the murmuring turned into grumbling. Althea's friends and admirers clearly weren't happy with this turn of events.

"I take it you didn't see this coming?" Jackson said as he leaned closer to speak into Liz's ear.

Liz's throat suddenly felt bone dry. "Not a clue, but I should have."

They both returned their attention to the women under the bright light.

"How *dare* you interrupt my speech," Althea huffed.

"Why don't you tell everyone how you've been lying about your own family history?" Julie said with a sweeping gesture to the audience.

Althea bit back. "What are you talking about?"

"Your ancestor John Ashby killed his first wife, Emma Hartsfeld Ashby, after learning she was in love with another man."

Someone uttered a cry of disapproval, and whispers filled the room.

Liz dropped her forehead into her hand. "Oh no."

"Now things are getting interesting," Jackson drawled.

"You don't know what you're talking about!" Althea volleyed back.

"I know enough to prove you're an academic fraud," Julie said. "All of your historical papers should be reviewed for authenticity."

Althea's outrage seemed to fill the room causing her supporters to rally to her side. The room got decidedly more vocal as murmurs turned into exclamations.

The president shook off his shock and spoke up. "Who are you to accuse someone with Dr. Mitchell's reputation and credentials?"

Julie preened for a moment and held out her hand. "Julie Sonders, soon to be published. I'm also available for speaking engagements."

"Which you'll never get by bad-mouthing me," Althea informed her.

"Really? You're one to talk. Tell Mr. Kenyon about how you've been trying to cover for your murderous ancestor."

"I have done no such thing." Althea's features darkened.

"Ladies, please." Mr. Kenyon tried to control the situation.

The women ignored him and continued squabbling. Liz rose and dropped her napkin to the table, ready to intervene. She'd made it to the bottom step of the dais when Althea cried out, "New information may have recently been discovered about my family, but that's far from a crime. *You*, however, should be arrested for poisoning me!"

Liz froze.

"I am not poisoning your reputation if what I say is true." Julie stood firm.

"You poisoned *me*!" Althea cried. "That's why I ended up in the hospital."

"What?" Julie's mouth gaped. "How dare you accuse me of poisoning you!"

"It wasn't until you started hanging around town that I had problems with my medicine. How do you explain that?"

Looking utterly confused by this turn of events, Julie took a step back. "Why would I touch your medicine?"

"To make me sick and to make me look incompetent. You wanted to destroy my good name to better your agenda." Althea glanced down at the table where her husband stood watching the exchange. "Herbert. Call the police."

Liz hurried up the steps. "Julie, you should probably get down."

Julie spun around to face Liz. "I didn't touch Dr. Mitchell's medicine!"

"Someone did," Althea said.

Realization colored Julie's face. She turned her head toward the crowd. Liz looked in that direction as well, just in time to see Lesley making her way across the room.

"Stop that woman!" Julie cried out. "She's the one who switched Dr. Mitchell's medicine."

Jackson swiftly headed off Lesley, barring the door before the young woman could exit.

"You have no right to keep me here," Lesley protested.

"You're not going anywhere," Jackson said.

Furious, Lesley turned and stormed toward Julie. "Just keep your mouth shut!"

"No way. I didn't hurt Dr. Mitchell. I'm not taking the blame."

Lesley's face turned red. "You're in this as much as I am."

"You never said anything about hurting anyone," Julie sputtered. She turned to Liz. "We just wanted information, that's all."

Stunned, Liz could hardly believe what she was hearing. She managed to find her voice and asked, "Information for what?"

Red blotches blossomed on Julie's cheeks. "Lesley found out about Frederick Hardy when she was working on another Civil War research project. She was fascinated by his claims and wanted the entire story, so she managed to get Dr. Mitchell to hire her. She knew I needed academic credit, so she included me, promising we'd both make names for ourselves when this was over. That's why she suggested you get in touch with me when you started digging into Emma's story."

Althea climbed down the steps. "You're my assistant, Lesley. Why would you do this to me?"

"Do you think I wanted this crummy job?" Lesley scoffed, her face twisting into an ugly expression. "I'm writing a true-life crime story featuring the Ashby family."

At hearing Lesley's intended purpose, Althea paled.

"Which I was *supposed* to be part of," Julie spat and the two started arguing again.

Liz edged back toward her table.

The main door opened and in walked Chief Houghton and Officer Dixon.

"Finally," Mary Ann said in relief. "The authorities are here."

Caitlyn sat back in her chair and took a drink. "Just another Saturday night in Pleasant Creek."

"And here I thought this banquet would be boring," Naomi admitted.

"Pity the police arrived so soon," Sadie said as she watched the action playing out before her. "This has to be the best dinner theater I've ever been to."

22

The Material Girls regrouped at the inn after the commotion died down. Sadie filled in Mrs. Hastings about the night's drama while the others readied tea and sliced the blueberry pie Mary Ann had baked. Then they camped around the dining room table to assess and decompress.

"What a night," Mary Ann said, a dazed expression still on her face.

"I don't know why anyone thinks Pleasant Creek is dull," Caitlyn commented.

Naomi chuckled. "After tonight, that myth will be put to rest."

"I know I plan to visit multiple times a year," Mrs. Hastings said before taking a sip of tea.

"Never a dull moment," Liz agreed, holding up a forkful of pie. "I have to admit, that's partly what I love about this town."

There were nods all around at that.

"Tell me, Liz," Sadie said, "did you suspect Julie had a part in all of this?"

"I knew she was ambitious, but I had no idea to what extent she'd go to dethrone Althea."

"How do you think she learned about John's supposed part in Emma's death?" Mary Ann's brow wrinkled at the question. "Did you have a chance to tell her after you met with Bert?"

"No, but she knew I was going to see Bert. I'm guessing she paid him a visit when she didn't hear back from me."

"Why would Bert tell her anything?" Caitlyn asked.

"He knew we were working together, so he probably didn't see any harm in telling her what we'd uncovered." Liz sighed. "She also apologized for *borrowing* the things she stole from me. She wanted copies to use later as proof for her all-important academic paper."

"And Clara's box?"

"Lesley took that. She confessed to Chief Houghton before he even got her in the patrol car. Jackson and I witnessed it."

"Who would have thought those girls were behind Althea's troubles?" Opal lifted a forkful of pie, but instead of taking a bite, set it back down on the plate. "Lesley acted like she cared about Althea."

"She and Julie only cared about themselves," Naomi surmised. "Sad."

"So what becomes of Emma's legacy?" Mary Ann asked.

"She certainly deserves better than what she received at the hands of John Ashby," Liz said. "Emma should be honored for her military service and all she went through."

"And so should you, Liz, for sticking with her." Sadie held up her cup. "You brought the truth to light."

"We all did," Liz said.

The women raised their cups.

Beans waddled into the kitchen, blinking at the group.

Liz held up her cup. "Here's to Beans. For unearthing the truth about Emma Hartsfeld Ashby."

Sensing the attention, Beans woofed.

"My hero," Liz said with a smile as the group laughed.

EPILOGUE

A month later, Liz was hurrying down the stairs with a basket of laundry when she heard a knock at the utility-room door. She answered to find the police chief waiting for her.

"We have to stop meeting like this," she deadpanned.

Chief Houghton chuckled. "I have some news I wanted to deliver to you in person."

"C'mon in."

The chief stepped inside.

Liz placed the basket on the washing machine and regarded him expectantly. "What's up?"

"I got the lab report back on your bones."

Liz's stomach flipped. "And?"

"The bones are Emma Ashby's. And, as you suspected, arsenic was detected in the remains."

Although Liz felt sad for Emma, it was a relief to finally get confirmation of her theory.

"Still, it doesn't prove that John Ashby intentionally killed her," the chief said.

"It's too late for that anyway," Liz reasoned. "I was more concerned with the identity of the remains. Now we know."

"If it hadn't been for Peter Cummings giving us the hair sample, we wouldn't be having this conversation."

After the drama of the awards banquet had died down, Liz insisted Althea and Clara have a long talk. They agreed and met at Althea's home. At Liz's request, Clara brought up Frederick's pocket watch. Althea checked the one in her collection and found the initials *FPH* engraved on the back. It had been Emma's keepsake from Frederick.

Althea had agreed to return it to Frederick's family and contacted Peter, who made the trip north to collect the family heirloom. After learning what had happened to the woman his ancestor had loved until his dying day, Peter showed them the locket Frederick had kept with him all his life. Inside was a lock of Emma's hair. With Althea's encouragement, he gave the sample to Chief Houghton, who then sent it to the lab.

"So will the remains be released to Althea?"

"With this positive ID, yes. But Dr. Mitchell and Mr. Cummings talked it over and decided Emma's remains should be reinterred beside Frederick." He sent her a curious look. "Did you have anything to do with that decision?"

Liz smiled. "I might have made a suggestion."

After the lock of hair had been found, Liz visited Althea. She knew she didn't have any right asking, but she'd implored Althea, legal custodian because Emma had been an Ashby, to let Emma spend eternity beside the man she had truly loved. Since the day Emma's remains had been found on the inn property, Liz had felt a responsibility toward the woman she had never met but had come to know. Althea had wholeheartedly agreed.

"Well, I'll be on my way." The chief started for the door and stopped. "I expect it to be business as usual around here from now on."

"Oh, Chief, haven't you heard? It's official that Pleasant Creek isn't a sleepy little town anymore. There's bound to be more excitement around the corner."

"Just as long as your dog doesn't dig up any more bones," he said as he exited.

Liz laughed to herself as she loaded the washing machine. When she was finished, she went back to the kitchen, nearly colliding with Clara.

"Liz. A moment?"

"Is something wrong?"

Clara fiddled with her purse strap. "You know that Althea and I set out to clear up the truth about the Ashby incident."

When the truth about Althea's family became known, she was actually in more demand than ever. Local groups wanted to hear the story and a television production company even approached her, wanting to film an episode about her family drama and how it had come to light. From the beginning, Althea had been afraid the truth about Emma would hurt her reputation. Instead, Emma had propelled Althea into the spotlight, and despite Emma not being a blood relative, Althea still wanted to pursue the contribution Emma had made during the war.

Julie hadn't been charged, but after how she'd behaved, her name wouldn't amount to much in academic circles. Liz certainly wouldn't give her a recommendation. Lesley was under investigation for tampering with Althea's medication, as well as breaking and entering Clara's house and Liz's room.

"There's more?" Liz asked in disbelief.

Clara nodded. "I wanted to tell Althea, but once you hear what I have to say, you'll understand why I kept this last part of the Parks's vow from her."

"It sounds serious."

"There's a reason Beans found Emma's remains on your property."

Liz narrowed her eyes. "I thought you didn't know she was buried here."

"I didn't," Clara said quickly. "Not exactly. According to family records, John buried Emma in the family plot after she died. Since they were all led to believe she succumbed to her illness, it was only natural she would rest in the Ashby cemetery."

"I'm getting a very bad feeling about this," Liz said.

"After John remarried and Emma became an afterthought to most people, he secretly had her remains removed from the family plot and buried elsewhere." Clara swallowed. "My family didn't know where for sure."

"We know now."

"You see why I couldn't tell Althea? It was bad enough John was a murderer, but to dig Emma up and move her?" Clara shuddered. "No one should suspect a family member of such a grisly deed."

"I agree. I won't say a word to Althea."

"Thank you, Liz."

After Clara left, Liz became restless. She went outside and was inevitably drawn to the lilac bushes she loved so much. Taking a seat on the bench, she tried not to dwell on the detestable final act against Emma. Instead, she concentrated on how grateful she was that she'd been able to persuade Althea to have Emma buried beside her true love.

"We all deserve a peaceful resting place," she said to Beans who had settled by her legs and was enjoying Liz's attention.

He looked up at her, as if to agree, and then wandered into the shade of her willow tree. She expected him to settle in for his tenth nap that day, but he surprised her by sniffing the ground and then digging furiously.

"Hey, stop it. Beans! No more digging." Liz jumped up and ran toward her wayward animal. He stopped, woofed in her direction, and went back to digging.

When she reached him, he got distracted from his quest. Liz was able to guide him back toward the inn. His front paws were caked with dirt, and Liz saw another bath in his near future. She unrolled the hose and turned on the water while Beans waited patiently, his head cocked to the side.

"Oh Beans," she said. "You're a good boy. But we don't need any new discoveries . . . at least not this week."

Up to this point, we've been doing all the writing. Now it's *your* turn!

Tell us what you think about this book, the characters, the bad guy, or anything else you'd like to share with us about this series. We can't wait to hear from *you*!

Log on to give us your feedback at:
https://www.surveymonkey.com/r/AmishInn

Annie's FICTION